MY BROTHER THE WEREWOLF

CRY WOLF!

You'll be howling for more
My Brother the Werewolf!

Puppy Love
Coming in 2013

Sienna Mercer

CRY WOLF!

J
FIC
MER
(series)

EGMONT

With special thanks to Stephanie Burgis

EGMONT
We bring stories to life

My Brother the Werewolf: Cry Wolf! first published in Great Britain 2013
by Egmont UK Limited
The Yellow Building, 1 Nicholas Road, London W11 4AN

Copyright © Working Partners Ltd 2013
Created by Working Partners Limited, London WC1X 9HH

ISBN 978 1 4052 6438 9

3 5 7 9 10 8 6 4 2

www.egmont.co.uk

A CIP catalogue record for this title is available from the British Library

Typeset by Avon DataSet Ltd, Bidford on Avon, Warwickshire
Printed and bound in Great Britain by the CPI Group

53024/3

EGMONT

Our story began over a century ago, when seventeen-year-old
Egmont Harald Petersen found a coin in the street. He was on
his way to buy a flyswatter, a small hand-operated printing
machine that he then set up in his tiny apartment.

The coin brought him such good luck that today Egmont has
offices in over 30 countries around the world. And that lucky
coin is still kept at the company's head offices in Denmark.

For Dave and Ben, with love

Chapter One

Bright summer sunshine streamed through the windows of Daniel Packer's bedroom, but the *last* thing he wanted to do was to go outside. 'Only for you, twin.' Sighing, he carefully laid his electric guitar on his bed. 'You've got a half-hour, but then I have to get back to my writing.'

'Awesome.' Tossing his football from hand to hand, Justin ran ahead to the stairs and jumped down the last five steps. 'Just don't feel bad when I run rings around you, OK?' he joked, opening the front door and running out. 'You may be the king of guitar, but when it comes to football: *I* rule!'

Daniel followed him into the front yard and couldn't help laughing as he watched his identical twin make a mock touchdown on the grass, and then follow it up with a full-on victory strut. 'Save it for the fans, dude.'

Justin grinned and pointed the football towards the far corner of the yard. 'Just head over there, OK? We're going to run some drills . . .'

Justin might as well have been speaking in a foreign language for all Daniel understood:

'. . . some hooks and ladders . . . post-patterns . . .'

You're talking to the wrong guy, Daniel thought, and shook his head. *I barely even know what a 'drill' is!* He didn't say a word, though. He knew better than to interrupt Justin when he was getting in *'the zone'.*

Even though his twin talked a good game, Daniel had seen Justin's panic grow over the last few days. He was seriously freaked about tomorrow's try-outs. So Daniel was going to ignore the fact that he couldn't care less about football: if his twin needed his help, he'd step up.

He caught a pass from Justin, and was raising the football to throw it back when he saw a familiar, tall, preppy girl armed with many, *many* clipboards heading down the street. 'Hey, look . . .' he said, lowering his arm. 'It's Riley.'

'Where?' Justin whipped around.

Daniel bit back a grin. 'Don't freak out,' he said. 'I bet she'll only sign you up for five or six different committees this time.'

Justin muttered something under his breath but Daniel didn't catch the words. He was already walking forwards. 'Hey, Riley!'

'Daniel!' Riley waved so enthusiastically she dropped her clipboards. 'Oops!' She bent over to gather them up – and four gel pens fell out of her shirt pocket, clattering on to the pavement.

Daniel fought back a laugh as he watched her gather all the things she'd dropped, her legs nearly tangling along the way. Riley had grown six inches in the last year, and now she was like a puppy tripping on oversized paws.

When she straightened, though, she looked as neatly put together as ever in her perfectly ironed top and plaid skirt, a plain black headband holding back her blonde hair. 'What are you doing holding a football, Daniel Packer?' she said. 'Isn't that more Justin's thing?'

'Yeah, well . . .' Daniel turned around to point an accusing finger at Justin, but the front yard was empty. *Where did he go?*

Was Justin hiding from Riley?

'Weird . . .' Daniel decided to change tack. 'What about you? School hasn't even started yet, and you're carrying, what, fifteen clipboards?'

Riley rolled her eyes. 'It's only six.'

Daniel grinned at her, shaking his head.

'Seriously, Riley. That's pretty epic organising, even for you.'

'School starts *tomorrow*, Daniel. There isn't much time left!' Riley waved her stack of clipboards at him. 'I'm supposed to be chairing three different clubs, but almost no one has signed up!'

He stared at her. 'That's because it's *sum-mer*. Remember? The time when we don't have to think about school.'

'Well, it's time for that to change,' Riley declared. 'Starting with you! Now, you were in the choral society last year – will you be signing up again?' She held out her top clipboard with a hopeful look.

Daniel pushed the clipboard gently away. 'Sorry, I'm concentrating on my own music this year.'

Riley frowned. 'Your own music?'

'My band – In Sheep's Clothing,' he said, his mind drifting back to his room, where his guitar was waiting. 'It's going to be great – even better once we get a singer. I'm holding auditions tomorrow.'

'Really?' Riley's voice suddenly sounded different – almost squeaky.

Before Daniel could ask her what was up, a large moving truck turned on to the street, its engine so loud it drowned out every other thought. It parked in the driveway of the house opposite his.

Finally, we have new neighbours.

The door of the truck opened. A girl about their age jumped out – and Daniel's breath caught in his throat. He thought he might have heard Riley asking something about his band's auditions, but he wasn't really paying attention to anything but the new girl. She wore a bright blue tank top and pale pink shorts, and her long, curly red hair glinted in the sunshine. When she turned and saw Daniel, she waved.

Daniel's mind went completely blank. Her smile was sort of . . . dazzling. He knew that there was something he should do in response – wave back, maybe? – but all he could do was stand there . . . staring.

And probably not in a 'cool' way.

'Daniel?' Riley prompted. 'The auditions? For your band? Never mind. I have recruiting to do!'

Waving her clipboards, she ran across the street. Her chunky-heeled shoe caught on a crack in the tarmac, nearly tripping, but this time she managed to catch herself without dropping anything. 'Hi!' she called out to the girl. 'Will you be attending Pine Wood Junior High? Want to sign up for one of my clubs?'

Daniel smiled. *Riley could definitely teach classes in determination!*

He was still standing there, watching her introduce herself to the new girl, when the football was scooped out of his arms. Justin was back.

'You!' Daniel turned on his twin. 'Where did you disappear to just now? I thought you were desperate to practise?'

'Yeah, well . . .' Justin shrugged and tossed the football in the air. He shot a quick glance across the street at Riley and the new girl. 'I just had to . . . check something.'

'What?' Daniel asked.

If Justin answered, Daniel didn't hear it. His gaze was drawn back across the street by the sound of the new girl's laughter. It was bright, it was *musical* –

Justin elbowed him in the ribs. 'So, there's a girl in the new family, huh?'

'I wasn't staring!' Daniel blurted. Then he winced as he heard his brother snicker. Daniel felt his face heat up as he forced himself to look away. 'I was just hoping – I mean, *wondering* – whether she'll be going to our school.'

'Yeah? Well, I just hope she's not like the last girl who lived there.'

They both shuddered. Mackenzie Barton had lived on their street for years, and ruled as their school's queen bee for even longer. Daniel and Justin had held a private celebration when the Bartons had finally moved house.

'No one could be as stuck-up as Mackenzie,' Daniel said. His gaze drifted back across the street, and he finished silently, *Especially not someone with a smile like that!*

'Hey, boys.' Behind them, the front door of their house opened and their dad stepped out, still wearing running shorts from his morning jog. 'How's the practice going?'

Their mother followed him, wearing a loose, floating summer dress. She looked across the street, raising one hand to shield her eyes against the sun. 'New neighbours?'

'That girl looks about your age,' Dad said. He

put one hand on Justin's shoulder. 'Isn't that your friend Riley she's talking to? You two should go over and introduce yourselves – welcome her to the neighbourhood.'

'OK!' Daniel said. He started forwards.

'Wait!' Justin caught his arm, looking panicked. 'Not now . . .' He flashed a quick look across the street at Riley and the new girl as they stood laughing together, while two adults were directing furniture on to the front lawn.

'Justin's right,' said Mom. 'I think they have more than enough to do already. Maybe we can invite them round for a barbecue in a few days, once they've settled in.'

'Yeah.' Justin nodded. 'What Mom said.'

His mom turned to Daniel and he had to dodge quickly to avoid a hair-tousle. 'I heard you practising upstairs,' she said to him. 'Your composition style is coming along wonderfully.'

'Thanks, Mom,' he said. 'Would be even

better —' he raised his eyebrows — 'if I had a new guitar.'

His mom gave a knowing grin as she went back inside.

Daniel turned to their dad, determined to get his point across. 'So, *Dad*,' he said firmly, 'where did you go this morning, before your jog? Mom said you had something "important" to do, but she wouldn't tell us what.'

Dad scooped the football out of Justin's hand and executed some perfect twirls of his own. 'Oh, I've been busy . . . uh . . . planning something.'

'*Something?*' Daniel tapped his fingertips together. 'Would that be . . . something for our birthday tomorrow?'

'Maybe,' Dad said. He traded a quick look with Justin. 'Let's not talk about it right now, OK? Quick, catch!' He threw the football across the grass in a tight, spinning arc, and Justin raced to catch it.

11

'Ohh-kay . . .' Daniel said, eyes widening. Surely his parents couldn't have missed all of the forty-thousand hints he'd dropped about the new guitar he'd seen in the town music store? Daniel swallowed hard. Just the thought of that guitar – a sleek V-shape in gleaming red – made his fingers itch to start playing. 'Come on, Dad,' he said. 'Can't you at least give me a hint? Was it –'

'Everything's fine!' Dad said. 'But, uh . . . I have some things to . . . *take care of.*'

Daniel swung to face Justin as their dad disappeared back inside the house. 'Do you know –'

'We're wasting practice time.' Justin cut him off, shoving the football into his arms. 'Come on! Let's try some passes, OK?'

Daniel waited until Justin was at the far end of the lawn, then threw the football to him as hard as he could.

'Whoa!' Justin leaped up to make the catch. Then he stared at Daniel as he shook out his hand where the football had hit it. 'That was . . . impressive. You haven't been faking all those music lessons, have you?'

'Just because I'm not a jock, doesn't mean I can't throw a ball,' Daniel said.

Shrieks of delight sounded from across the street. Riley and the new girl were both jumping up and down with excitement. *Looks like Riley has a new recruit!*

Then Daniel realised he had an opening line. All he had to do was call out, casually, 'Be careful of Riley, she'll sign you up to –

'Argh!' Daniel cried as a blast of pain exploded in his chest. He staggered back, fumbling for the ball that Justin must have thrown while Daniel was looking – *not* staring – at the new girl.

His fingers slipped. He batted the ball in the air, trying to keep it in his grip . . . and then his

13

feet slipped, too, sending him backwards on to the grass with a thud.

Giggles drifted over from across the street.

Cringing, he closed his eyes. *Real smooth, Daniel!*

The next moment, he heard footsteps, and his eyes snapped open. 'I'm fine!' he croaked. Grabbing the ball, he pushed himself up. *Can't let them think I've been hurt by a stupid football . . . even if I can barely breathe.*

At least Justin hadn't done one of his disappearing acts this time. He crossed the lawn to stand by Daniel, as Riley led the new girl towards them.

'This is Debi,' Riley announced. 'She's just moved here from a little town called Franklin Grove. And she's in our grade! Isn't that great?'

Daniel was fighting so hard to breathe normally, he couldn't reply. So he just smiled and lifted his hand in a wave. Then he put it back down because he thought it was probably dorky to wave at someone who was less than five feet away.

'Hi,' Justin mumbled, sounding as winded as Daniel felt.

Then came an awkward silence.

Come on, Justin, Daniel silently begged his twin. *Make conversation!*

'Aaaaaaanyway!' Riley said, raising an eyebrow. 'I have to go. So many clubs; so little time.'

'Right.' Suddenly Justin seemed to breathe a lot easier. 'Nice to see you, Riley.' Then he winced as if he'd said something embarrassing.

At least he said something, *which is better than I'm doing,* Daniel thought.

As Riley walked away, Debi turned her smile to Justin. 'You're pretty good at football.'

'Thanks.' Justin grinned, snagging the ball from Daniel's arms. 'Have you seen many games?'

She laughed. 'I was a cheerleader at my old school, so yeah, *tons*. I watched you guys practising just now, and you've got great moves for a . . .' She stopped, wrinkling her nose in adorable confusion. 'How old are you?'

'Twelve. Well, twelve for one more day,' Justin said.

'That's right,' said a voice behind them. Mr Packer had stuck his head out of the living room window and was beaming with pride. 'It's a big day for Justin tomorrow . . . oh, and for Daniel, too.'

Daniel shook his head. *Why is Dad acting so weird? It is my birthday, too. If it wasn't, Justin and I wouldn't be twins.*

'Well, tomorrow's a cool day to have a birthday,' Debi said. 'It's a full moon tonight, and –'

'I know!' Dad smiled a toothy smile. Then he began to laugh . . . and laugh.

And laugh.

Daniel cringed with embarrassment. *Just please*

16

don't let him start up his favourite lecture . . .

'You know,' Dad began. *Too late,* Daniel thought. 'Historically, the full moon, and the lunar cycles in general, were hugely significant in every culture . . .'

Daniel's shoulders hunched as he tuned out the same old speech he'd heard a million times before; all about the moon, and how it 'waxed'. *What is waxing?* Blah, blah, neap tides . . . blah, blah, lunar eclipse . . .

Debi was smiling as she listened, her head tilted attentively. This just made Daniel feel even worse. *It's nice of her to pretend to be interested . . . but a crazy family is not the way to make a good impression.*

Of course, since he'd already gotten knocked on to the grass by a football – and then stood as silent as a stone while she'd tried to make small-talk – it was probably time to give up on making a good impression . . .

An *only half-bad* impression would have to do

at this point – as long as it wasn't an impression of a total idiot.

At long last, the torture ended when Dad turned to head back inside. 'Come with me, Justin, will you?'

'Aw, Dad.' Justin groaned.

'You can practise later,' Dad said. 'Right now, you and I need to talk.'

Sighing, Justin trudged over to the front door and into the house. Daniel felt a pang of sympathy. *Poor Justin. He's never going to get a chance to practise . . .*

. . . And then he realised the bigger problem.

Wait a minute. They can't leave me alone with Debi!

But there was no way out. Dad had his arm around Justin and was ushering him inside. The only thing left for Daniel to do was turn to face Debi, which he did – slowly.

Think, brain! Come on. There has to be something cool I can say!

Debi was looking at him with definite interest, but that just made Daniel's mind go even more blank. It was like the entire English language was falling out of his brain, word by word.

At least this time I won't fall on my butt in front of her . . . I hope.

Justin slumped in his seat, half-covering his eyes. *Dad's having a meltdown.*

His usually calm, controlled father was pacing back and forth in his study, practically vibrating with tension. 'I'm just so excited . . . so proud of you . . . so . . .' He pushed his hand through his hair until it stood up like the fur of an agitated German Shepherd.

'Chill, Dad,' Justin mumbled.

'Chill?' Dad let out a short bark of laughter. With shaking fingers, he punched the 'on' button of the stereo, and a second later the sound of violins floated into the air. Justin recognised

19

the sound of Mom's orchestra playing Dad's favourite piece, 'Song to the Moon'. The whole family had been forced to listen to that one an awful lot, lately.

A moment later, Dad lit the fat, pine-scented candles he kept on his bookcase.

'I can't help it,' he said. 'I'm so jittery about tonight, I might transform right here, right now!'

'Don't do that!' Justin jerked upright. 'Tonight is not that big a deal, Dad, OK? My first transformation may not even happen yet. Don't the rules say "the first full moon of the thirteenth year"? Tonight's full moon might not count, since it starts before my birthday.'

'I just have this *sense* —'

Justin jumped out of his own chair, too antsy to keep still. His dad was making him crazy! 'I don't know, Dad,' Justin said, beginning to pace the room himself. 'I read those books you gave me. When a kid is half-human and half-werewolf, there's only a fifty–fifty chance that the change will happen at all. I might *never* turn.'

Dad raised an eyebrow, looking amused. 'I know the statistics.' He sat down in the big chair behind his desk, smoothing down his ruffled hair. 'But, trust me, Justin – you're a natural.' He ticked off the points on his fingers as he explained: 'You're good at sports, you have quick reactions . . . *and* your thirteenth birthday is falling on a full moon!' He shook his head, grinning widely. 'I have a good feeling . . . It is *definitely* going to happen tonight!'

'Great,' Justin muttered. A wild pine fragrance floated up from the candles. *Am I really going to be running out there as a werewolf tonight?*

Between the two candles, an enamelled clay object rested on the shelf. It was a wolf's paw print. Justin looked down at it and swallowed hard.

'What about Daniel?' He turned back to his

dad. 'When are we going to tell him the truth?'

'Daniel . . .' For the first time, Dad seemed to lose some of his enthusiasm. 'Well, the thing is, your mother and I are just not sure about whether we *should* tell Daniel.'

'What do you mean?' Justin stared at him. 'Once I start turning, he's going to find out –'

'Not if you don't tell him,' Dad said flatly. 'And you need to think hard about this, Justin. When mixed human–werewolf parents have twins, only one will ever be able to go wolf. How will Daniel feel if he finds out about an amazing, secret world that he can never belong to?'

'Well . . .' Justin collapsed back on to the chair by Dad's desk. 'I guess . . .'

But this is the only secret I've ever kept from Daniel, he thought.

Somehow, he was no longer feeling all that excited about turning into a werewolf.

Daniel would have given anything to have his twin back in the yard with him. It might have only been seconds since Justin had left, but it felt like hours since either he or Debi had spoken. *I can't believe Dad and Justin both ditched me in my time of need.*

Debi smiled brightly at him.

Say something smart, you idiot! Daniel told himself, trying to remember how to inhale and exhale in the right order.

Unfortunately, the only thing he could think of to say to Debi was the fact that he couldn't think of anything to say. Probably not the best conversation-starter!

Debi's gaze slid down to the grass . . . where, Daniel realised, his foot was tapping nervously. He forced himself to be still. She cleared her throat, looked back at him . . .

Forget smart – just say anything!

'Um . . .' Daniel winced. *I can't stop now . . .*

'Sorry,' he mumbled. 'You know, about my dad going on about all that boring moon stuff.'

Debi shook her head. 'It's OK. I'm actually fascinated by astronomy.'

'Oh . . .' *I just accidentally called her boring!* 'Me, too! Fascinated. Not just "fascin", but completely "ated" as well.'

Debi smiled politely. Daniel grinned back and tried to look like he wasn't uncomfortable. Unfortunately, he didn't know how to pull that off – especially not when he was thinking about how stupid he must sound.

In the distance, birds chirped.

Debi broke the silence just before Daniel could break down and run. 'So . . . identical twins, huh?'

Daniel's shoulders relaxed. If there was one thing he had always had an easy time talking about, it was twins. 'Well, we might look identical, but actually, Justin's turning thirteen at 1.07 a.m., and I'm turning thirteen at 1.01. So, technically, I'm the older brother.'

Debi laughed, and Daniel felt his brain go fuzzy at the sound. *Don't mess this up now!*

'Seriously, though,' he said, 'we've always been close, even though we're pretty different. Justin's into sports – you could probably tell – and I've got my band: *In Sheep's Clothing.*'

Debi tilted her head, looking thoughtful. 'There were identical twins at my old school at Franklin Grove. They were girls, but a lot like you two – totally different, but both cool.'

Daniel's jaw dropped open. 'Really?' he blurted. Then he cringed. *Why did I say that? Cool people aren't* surprised *that they're cool! That wouldn't be cool.*

'Uh-oh.' Debi pointed to the house across the street, where her parents were waving to her. 'Looks like I can't avoid unpacking forever.'

She started across the lawn, then looked back

over her shoulder, her blue eyes vivid in the sunlight. 'I'll see you at school tomorrow, Daniel.'

'Yeah,' Daniel said. 'Tomorrow.'

Debi's long, curly red hair bounced around her as she crossed the street, and Daniel had to force himself to snap his mouth shut.

Suddenly, he was really looking forward to the start of school.

Chapter Two

The clock on Justin's bedside table read 12.58 a.m., but there was no way he was going to sleep. In just nine more minutes, it would be 1.07 a.m. and, after all the years of waiting, finally time for him to fulfil his family destiny by becoming a –

'Argh!'

His dad clicked the door open and poked his head round. 'Ready, buddy?'

No! Justin thought. But at the same time, his skin prickled with sudden excitement. It was finally *happening*.

He nodded, unable to speak, and followed

his dad out of the room.

As they tiptoed downstairs Justin wiped his sweaty hands on his pyjama shorts. 'Uh, Dad?' He had to clear his throat before he could keep going. 'How does it actually . . . *feel*?'

'Well . . .' Dad laid one hand reassuringly on Justin's shoulder as they walked through the kitchen to the French doors. 'First, there's an itching sensation. That part might be uncomfortable for a bit. Then, after that, your teeth will start to tingle like you've eaten too much sugar.' His dad slid back the doors and stepped out into the night.

'Got it.' Justin ran his tongue behind his teeth. *That doesn't sound so bad.*

Outside, on the patio, Justin looked up to the night sky. Clouds had covered the full moon, and the backyard was full of shadows. An owl hooted close by, and Justin gave a nervous start.

'And that's when everything starts to get good!' Dad said. He grinned and gave Justin's shoulder a friendly shake. 'Not only will you grow claws, your sense of smell and hearing will be heightened like never before. It's incredible. Then your hair will grow, and –'

Dad's voice cut off as the clouds parted overhead. The light of the full moon bathed the yard in silver light.

Justin didn't need an alarm clock to tell him what time it was.

1.07 a.m. Game time.

He braced himself. *I can do this. I've been waiting my whole life for it.*

Moonlight shimmered over his arms until his skin seemed to glow. *Is that an itch on my shoulder?* Justin swallowed hard, feeling the nerves in his arms leap to attention. *Yes! That's definitely an . . .*

Oh. He rolled his shoulder. It felt fine.

So, it hadn't started yet. *OK, well, maybe my leg!* He shifted position hopefully – then realised that the itch he'd felt was just a dandelion poking against his ankle.

Justin scowled. *Will it all hurry up and* happen *already?*

The moon was still lighting up his skin . . . but maybe the change would happen when he least expected it. Justin closed his eyes and forced his muscles to relax. *Ohh-kaay. I'm just standing outside . . . in the dark . . . in my pyjamas . . . just like any other totally normal thirteen year-old boy. I'm really not expecting aaaanything right now . . .*

A shadow fell across his closed eyelids. He opened them – and saw that clouds had shifted to cover the moon again.

Hmm.

Slowly, reluctantly, he turned. 'Dad?' Justin peered through the darkness, but he could only just make out his dad's face.

It had an expectant look. 'Son?'

Justin swallowed hard, then admitted: 'I don't feel any different.'

I'm still completely human. And that means . . .

As his stomach twisted, Justin couldn't meet his dad's eyes any more. 'I'm sorry,' he mumbled.

There was a horrible moment of silence. Then . . .

'Don't be ridiculous.' Dad gave his shoulder a hearty slap. A hearty slap that kind of hurt. '*I* should be apologising for getting us both all worked up, thinking tonight would be the night.' Dad looped his arm around Justin's shoulders and started guiding him back towards the house. 'It's my fault. You were right before – it will happen at the next full moon.' He started to tousle Justin's hair – then stopped to finger its length.

Justin jerked away. 'I *told* you, it's not growing!'

'Of course not! Only to be expected. We have *plenty* of time.' As Dad slid open the door to the house, he dropped his voice to a whisper. 'Sorry, kiddo. I'm just so thrilled that you'll be carrying on our great werewolf tradition . . . later this month.'

'Later this month,' Justin repeated. He shook his head. Now that the excitement had drained away, his whole body felt heavy with exhaustion. All he wanted was to go to bed and forget that this had ever happened.

'I can't wait to share it all with you. As soon as – huh.' Dad stopped part-way through the door, frowning and cocking his head. 'Did you hear something?'

'Nope.' Justin shook his head, trudging up the stairs. 'I don't have super-hearing like you. Not yet.'

'I guess not.' Dad sighed and followed after him. 'It was probably just one of the other wolves in town, howling at the full moon.'

Justin froze on the top step. *'The other wolves in town . . .' Oh, no!*

The football try-outs!

Coach Johnston was a werewolf. *And* he'd

been signing up guys with werewolf heritage to play Offense. Dad had been so sure Justin would turn wolf by tomorrow that Justin had promised Coach Johnston that he would make the change in time for the start-of-year try-outs.

Without the speed and agility of a full werewolf, though . . .

Justin wanted to tip his head back and howl his frustration at the moon, but he wasn't a wolf, and his throat didn't work that way.

This is going to be a disaster.

Daniel could not get comfortable in his bed. He figured it had to be almost 1 a.m. by now, but he still hadn't managed to fall asleep. A new melody was stuck in his brain, playing over and over no matter how hard he tried to ignore it.

I give up. He clambered out of bed. *If I write it down, maybe then I'll be able to sleep.*

He turned on the light and grabbed a sheet

of paper. For once, the words came just as quickly as the music.

He even knew the title already: 'Moonlight Girl.' As he worked out the melody, he muttered the lyrics to himself.

'. . . a smile as bright as stars . . .'

'. . . hair that shines like fire . . .'

He'd never had a song come so easily before! He didn't know where it had come from, but he couldn't stop it pouring out of him.

As he grabbed another sheet, he heard a sound from outside. He glanced out the window: Justin was standing in the backyard, next to their dad. They were huddled together; it looked like a *serious* talk.

Daniel backed away from the window – if they looked up and saw him awake, they'd drag him down for their late-night football practice.

And he had a song to write.

The next line . . . Daniel scratched his head,

trying to think. The lyrics had been so clear until the noises from the backyard had distracted him, but now . . .

He scratched his arm. Then an itch started burning up his leg. *Drat! I shouldn't have petted Poochy next door. I knew he had fleas!*

His other leg began to itch, and he groaned.

As he scratched, Daniel caught sight of the glowing alarm clock in the corner of the room. *1.04 a.m.*

'Happy birthday to me, happy bir – argh!' He stopped singing as his teeth started to tingle. He probably shouldn't have eaten a donut before bed, but he'd still been hungry after dinner.

Sighing, he ran his tongue over his teeth.

'Ouch!' He clamped one hand to his mouth – and then, when he pulled it away, saw a smudge of blood on his finger.

He took a deep breath, trying to ignore the weird tingling sensations rippling all over his body.

Forget it. Just concentrate on the song.

He picked up his guitar. Then he froze, staring at his fingernails . . . which were suddenly so long, they overlapped the strings on the guitar.

Panic thrummed beneath his skin. *This has to be a bad dream.*

He dropped the guitar on the bed, trying not to let himself look at his hands. Then he hurried into the bathroom he shared with Justin. *I'll splash some water on my face. That'll wake me up.*

He opened the door to the darkened bathroom, nearly staggering because of an overwhelming smell of toothpaste. Had Justin spilled an entire *tube* in here?

Daniel winced, covering his ears with his hands. *And when did Mom's snoring get so LOUD?*

Forcing himself into the bathroom, he turned on the faucet and splashed cold water on his face – but something about the sensation felt . . . *different*. It was almost as if his face . . .

His stomach twisted in dread. He reached for the light switch – then stopped, squeezing his eyes shut.

Do I really *want to see this?*

He took a deep breath – and felt his teeth scrape against the inside of his lips. He shuddered as he reached for the light switch.

When the light came on, Daniel gasped as he stared at his own reflection in the mirror. He clamped one hand over his mouth . . . but it wasn't enough to stop the sound that came out:

'*Howwwwwwwwwwwwwwwwwwwwwl!*'

Chapter Three

The moment that Justin's alarm clock sounded, memories of the night before flooded his mind. Groaning, he pulled his pillow over his head.

What a disaster.

Then he remembered what Coach said when any of the team sulked. *Get a grip, cub!* Shaking his head, he smiled and mocked himself for being such a wuss. He might not be a full werewolf yet, but he was still thirteen today. It was time to find his twin for their favourite birthday tradition: *Pancake Piles!*

OK, maybe a heavy breakfast of pancakes

wasn't the smartest idea for the day of his football try-outs, but after last night, he definitely deserved it. And anyway, Daniel would never accept him skipping their birthday ritual.

'Where *is* Daniel, anyway?' For once, Justin didn't hear any sounds coming from his brother's room. Even when it wasn't their birthday, Daniel was usually up and out of bed before anyone else, like a . . . *um* . . . like that animal that made a loud racket in the morning?

Justin picked up the birthday card he'd gotten for Daniel and knocked on his brother's door . . . only to get a growl for a reply.

Justin frowned. Daniel wasn't usually grumpy in the mornings. Shrugging, he knocked again, then headed into the pitch-black room. 'Happy birthday, Bro! Ready for Pancake Piles?'

Silence.

'Oh, come on, dude.' Justin rolled his eyes.

'We're thirteen, not thirty! It's not a time for a midlife crisis.'

He snorted with laughter – then stopped, as he realised that Daniel wasn't joining in. 'Hey . . . that was *funny*.'

Still nothing.

Scowling, Justin stomped over to the window and pulled the curtains open. 'It's time to wake up, twin.' When he turned back, he saw that Daniel had his blanket over his head. Justin shook his head in disbelief. 'Seriously? What's up with you?'

'Nothing.' Daniel's grunt came out muffled by the blanket. 'Leave me alone.'

Justin stared at the lump under the covers. 'What's wrong?' When he didn't get any answer, he tried to work it out on his own. 'I know you were fine last night. So, what could have happened between then and now to . . .?'

He took a deep breath. *I should have known*

this would happen. 'Daniel?' he said. He sat down on the edge of Daniel's bed. 'Did you hear me going outside with Dad last night?' Justin licked his lips nervously. *I have to level with him . . . even if I can't tell him the whole truth.* 'I know it might seem strange that we didn't ask you to come with us, and I know Dad's been weird about the whole birthday thing, but . . . he does love us both equally, OK? It's just, I've got more in common with him. I like sports-stuff, like he does; you're more musical, like Mom. That's . . .' He sighed, looking down at his hands. 'That's all it is. Seriously.'

I hate lying to my twin brother.

Still, Justin thought he'd done a pretty good job. He'd been sensitive and caring, just like Mom was always telling him to be. No way any reasonable person could still be annoyed at him after *that* speech . . .

But judging by the total silence coming from

41

under the blanket, it hadn't done him any good at all with Daniel.

Just like last night, Justin had failed a member of his family.

'Forget it,' he mumbled, dropping Daniel's birthday card on to the bed and starting for the door. 'Just forget about our birthday, then. And forget about Pancake Piles. I don't want them any more.'

As his door closed, Daniel winced. He'd hated acting like such a jerk to Justin . . . but he'd had no choice. How could he tell his brother that he'd turned into some sort of freaky fur-boy?

Panic rippled through him all over again, making him feel dizzy and smothered in his blanket-cave. *I can't believe this is happening.*

First he'd cut his tongue on his teeth last night, then . . . *wait*. Daniel blinked. *My tongue doesn't hurt any more.* Bracing himself, he ran it over his teeth and . . .

They're back to normal!

Pushing off the blanket, Daniel stared down at his hands. His nails were just nails again – maybe not as short as they should be for guitar-playing, but nothing like they'd been last night.

Just one thing left. He took a deep breath.

Slowly, he reached up to feel his face.

It feels fine! He patted his cheeks and forehead. *Just skin! Normal!*

And that meant . . .

It was all just a dream. Just a weird, horrible dream!

Light-headed with relief, Daniel jumped out of bed, ran to the bathroom, and locked the door without turning on the light. He took a deep breath and flicked the light switch.

Pleasepleaseplease let it have been a dream!

He opened his eyes, and . . .

Completely normal. Daniel let out his breath. He headed back into his bedroom. Sunlight shone in through the windows, lighting up his *ordinary* bedroom. Nothing was scary, nothing was wrong, and he was absolutely fine. Just a totally normal twelve-year-old . . .

. . . No, not twelve – thirteen! Daniel's eyes landed on the birthday card at the end of his bed.

Uh-oh.

Justin must have brought the card in – before Daniel's bad mood had chased him away.

'Daniel!' his mom shouted from downstairs. 'Are you coming to breakfast, sweetie?'

Daniel scooped up the card, opened his door and raced down the stairs, taking them two at a time.

'Justin!' he yelled. 'Hey, Justin!'

He didn't hear any answer from his twin. But he grinned as he neared the kitchen and heard the clanking of pots and pans.

Oh, yeah, I'm ready for some birthday pancakes . . .
piles and piles of them!

An hour later, the twins were walking side by side up the front steps of Pine Wood Junior High School, and Justin was feeling better about everything. Even the thought of double physics that morning couldn't take away his birthday glow, now that his brother was out of his grump funk from earlier.

Beside him, though, Daniel frowned and stopped to stare at some new graffiti on the school sign. 'I don't get it. Why would anyone put a "Lu" in front of "Pine"?'

'Who knows?' Justin shrugged, trying to look innocent as he kept moving up the big stone steps. His twin might not understand, but 'lupine' meant 'wolf'. The werewolves at Pine Wood Junior High were making a statement . . . just in time for football try-outs.

45

His stomach twisted at the thought, but he shoved the panic down. *It's still my birthday – and the first day of school.* 'Come on, dude,' he said, gesturing for his brother to keep up. 'It's time to work out our schedules.'

'Right.' Daniel shrugged and caught up with him.

As they stepped into the big foyer, the twins moved to one side to huddle over their schedules. Streams of students rushed past them as they figured out their lockers and classrooms. The energy swirling through the air was so intense, it felt almost like game-time. Justin was totally digging the rush of adrenaline.

Until a much-too-familiar voice spoke behind him.

'There you are!' Mackenzie Barton was already wearing her cheerleading outfit, complete with a set of pom-poms that she shook at Justin threateningly. 'I've been looking for you everywhere!'

'Uh . . . you have?' Justin could feel Daniel easing away from his side. *Traitor!* He reached out to snag his twin's schedule, stuffing it under his arm to hold it hostage. *If I have to deal with the Queen of Mean, so do you!* 'What do you want, Mackenzie?'

'I just want you to know I have your cheer all worked out.' She looked smug. 'I went ahead and got them ready, you know, since I'm going to be Head Cheerleader this year.'

Daniel cleared his throat. 'I thought the cheerleading try-outs weren't until this afternoon.'

She rolled her eyes. 'Whatever! As if there was any doubt.'

'Don't count your chickens, Mackenzie,' Justin said. 'You might be named Head Cheerleader, but *I* might not get on to the football team.'

Mackenzie shook her head, making her glossy brown ponytail flick across her face.

'Don't be ridiculous. Everyone in this town thinks it's your year.'

Justin gulped. 'Yeah, well, everyone might be wrong.' He could feel beads of sweat popping up across his skin at the thought. 'Trust me . . . it is definitely not a foregone conclusion.'

Mackenzie's eyes narrowed. 'You'll be in *big* trouble if you don't make the team, after all the work I've put into your cheer. It took almost all summer! And not only that – you'd better be made running back! Do you have any idea how hard I had to work to find a rhyme that worked with *Packer*?'

With that, she flounced off, leaving Justin staring after her. Pine Wood's scariest brunette had struck again. Justin swallowed hard, feeling all his birthday joy fade away – and a whole load of stress and pressure flooding in to take its place.

Pine Wood had won the regional football championship the last four years in a row, mostly because of their carefully hidden secret: all the players on Offense, and most of the Defense were werewolves. That made them stronger and more naturally athletic than their opponents. Since most of the other guys who'd be joining the team today had already turned thirteen earlier in the year, they'd had plenty of time to get used to their werewolf powers.

Not me. All of a sudden, Justin felt cold and very alone despite the crowds of students swirling around him.

Then Daniel nudged his side. 'Wow, did you see that? She's sure taking a lot for granted.'

'What?' Justin blinked. Then he followed the direction of Daniel's pointing finger. The back of Mackenzie's cheerleading outfit read, *'Head Cheerleader'*, in big embroidered letters.

'Wow,' Justin echoed. 'She's really confident.'

I only wish I was, he thought.

He hadn't said the words out loud, but Daniel

seemed to hear them anyway. He slapped Justin on the back so hard that Justin staggered forwards. 'Don't worry, Bro. For once, Mackenzie's actually right about something. You're the best football player I know.'

Justin rolled his eyes. 'You don't even know any other football players, dude.'

'Exactly.' Daniel winked and scooped his schedule out from under Justin's arm. 'Oh, before I forget . . .' Daniel rummaged in his backpack for a wad of red and black paper. 'Do you think you could hang up a few of my posters on your way to Homeroom?'

'Why not?' Justin took the posters. 'Are these for your band's auditions?'

'They'll start right after your try-outs,' Daniel said, nodding. 'I just hope someone with real moves shows up. We need a good lead vocalist if we want to take our sound to the next level.'

Justin shrugged. 'How hard can it be to find a

singer? Hey, there's a whole choral society in this school.'

'Yeah, but can they rock?' Daniel sighed. 'I guess if it really came to it, I could sing *and* play guitar, but I'd rather just stick with the guitar.'

'Let's hope your posters pull in a star, then,' Justin said, glancing down at the blood-red lettering on the top poster.

Are you ready to Rock Out?
Are you willing to unleash your hidden BEAST?
In Sheep's Clothing *is looking for a new member!*

Justin had to smother a laugh. If only Daniel knew. There were so many beasts waiting to be unleashed in Pine Wood.

'Why are you grinning?' Daniel asked.

'Uh . . .' Justin's mind went blank. 'No reason!' he said. 'I just. . .'

There was a loud bang on the lockers behind them.

Thank goodness. Justin felt pure relief. *I don't have to explain!*

He turned to see what had made the noise, and nerves raced across his body like spreading sunburn. Riley. *Oh, no!* His gaze shot around, hunting for escape. *Why isn't there anywhere to hide in this hallway? What kind of school doesn't put in secret passageways for moments like this?*

But it was no use. Taking a deep breath, Justin forced a clenched-teeth grin on to his face.

She was charging towards them through the crowds with a smile that could have lit up the whole school. Justin barely even noticed her stack of textbooks and clipboards. All his focus was on the cute face that had been doing funny things to his knees since last year, when everything had changed.

Don't be stupid, he ordered himself. *She's just*

a friend. Justin and Daniel had been at the same school as Riley since kindergarten. She'd been in the choral society with Daniel for years, and she was the only person in town, other than their parents, who could properly tell the twins apart. She was as familiar as the houses in his neighbourhood.

But last year, Justin had started seeing her differently.

'So!' she said. As she skidded to a halt in front of them, papers fell to the ground all around her, but she didn't seem to notice. 'How are my favourite identical twins?'

'Um,' Justin choked. 'Urk . . .' *Oh, no. Now she probably thinks I'm having some kind of fit!* Quickly, he leaned over to start picking up Riley's papers. *At least this way she can't see my face.*

'Isn't it your birthday today?' Riley asked brightly.

'It sure is.' Daniel held up his stack of posters

as Justin straightened. 'But I've got twenty of these to put up before Homeroom starts, so I've got to take off. Now.'

'Oh.' Riley slumped, her smile fading.

'See you later, guys.' Daniel took off without a look back.

Justin held out Riley's papers to her – but she didn't even notice. She was too busy staring after Daniel.

Oh, no. Justin's stomach tightened as he took in her expression. She was definitely gazing after his brother with a wistful look.

Does she like Daniel?

He had to find out. 'So . . . what's up?' he asked, holding out her papers as casually as he could.

Unfortunately, it was a bit *too* casual. As she turned back, Riley knocked Justin's hand, sending the papers falling back to the ground – along with all her textbooks. 'Ouch!' she yelped, as the heaviest book landed on her toes.

Hopping on one leg, she reached down to hold her injured foot, and knocked straight into a seventh grader.

'Sorry!' Cringing, Justin knelt back down to start picking her papers and textbooks up again.

'Nothing's up,' Riley said softly, accepting the bundle from Justin. 'I was just hoping to . . . *talk* . . . to Daniel.'

'Talk?' Justin's voice came out strangled. *What did all those pauses mean?* She'd paused before saying Daniel's name! And before the word 'talk'!

She likes my brother. His stomach suddenly tightened into a knot.

Get a grip, cub! He barked the silent order at himself. *Do* not *show your feelings!*

He cleared his throat. 'So. You wanted to talk to Daniel.' *There. That sounded totally normal. Not at all like I'm panicking. Which I'm not. Absolutely.*

Riley was blushing as she squeezed her pile of books and clipboards closer to her body.

'Yeah. You know.' She nodded at the posters in Justin's hand. 'The auditions.'

It's not Daniel! It's just the band! Justin let out a laugh of pure surprise. 'Wait, *you* want to be their lead singer?'

Riley frowned. 'Why do you ask in *that* voice?'

'Well . . .' Justin shrugged, looking from her preppy clothes to the stack of textbooks and clipboards in her arms. 'I just don't see you as a rock-girl type. You know, "unleashing the hidden beast" and all that.'

'Why not?' Justin sensed annoyance in her narrowing eyes.

'Well, you know. You're kind of . . . you know . . .'

'Kind of *what?*' Now Riley's tone was as cold as ice. She stared at him.

'You know . . .' Justin winced.

Stop saying, 'You know,' because – clearly – you don't!

'Never mind.' She snatched a poster from

56

Justin's pile. 'Thanks for sharing your real opinion of me.'

'I . . . I . . .?'

But it was too late. Riley was already storming off, with that slightly awkward gait that was so adorable it made Justin's brain go fuzzy.

Now all he wanted to do was kick himself. *Great work, doofus. Couldn't you have at least finished your sentence?* His shoulders sagging, he finished it in his own head. *'You're kind of . . . nice.'*

A millisecond later, every thought was knocked out of his brain as five boys smashed into him with the force of a truck, knocking him back against the wall of lockers.

'Happy beastly birthday, *dawg!*'

It was the five jocks who made up the football team's core Offense – universally known as "the Beasts", for more reasons than most kids at Pine Wood really knew.

'Ow!' Justin tried to stifle his cry of pain, but

he couldn't cut it off entirely. That *hurt*.

The Beasts laughed when they heard it.

'"*Ow!*" Good one!' Kyle Hunter, the leader, pounded his shoulder approvingly with one meaty fist. 'As if a Lupine like you could get hurt!'

'Ha,' Justin said. 'Yeah.' Wincing, he rolled out his shoulder where Kyle had slammed into it. 'Classic.'

'So?' Ed Yancey, Kyle's right-hand man, pounded Justin's other shoulder with a delighted grin. 'Did it happen last night, like you thought?'

'Uh . . .'

'How does it feel?' Chris Jordan chimed in. 'Are you ready to take on The Tigers?'

'The Tigers . . .' Justin felt his breathing speed up at the thought. The Tigers were Pine Wood's main rivals – and the two teams would be squaring off in the year's first football game, in just one week.

58

And Justin was not going to be a werewolf for another *month!*

He faked a laugh, feeling sick. 'Bunch of wimps,' he said. 'They don't scare me.'

The Beasts all laughed approvingly, launching another avalanche of celebratory punches. Justin forced his grin to stay in place. 'But guys,' he said, 'I haven't even made the team yet. So . . .'

'Dude!' Kyle shook his head. 'You making the team is a foregone conclusion. Everyone knows what a great athlete you've always been, and that was *before*. If you were that good already, just imagine how good you'll be now that you're . . .' He broke off, looking left and right. Then he leaned in and whispered, his breath stinking of bacon: '. . . full *wolf!*'

Standing frozen, Justin felt like a mouse caught in a cat's paw. 'Right,' he said. 'Full wolf. Just like you guys. Totally.'

'Let me tell you, man, we are *all* looking forward to watching your try-out,' Kyle said. Stepping back, he gave a high-five that nearly knocked Justin's arm out of its socket. 'See ya after school, dude.'

'See ya,' Justin repeated faintly.

He watched the Beasts walk away down the hall, a mass of muscle and predatory strength.

Keep cool, he ordered himself.

Despite the aching bruises where they'd pounded him, Justin didn't let himself gulp or fall back against the lockers. He knew they'd be able to hear both of those giveaways with their werewolf senses, even from all the way down the hall.

Inside, though, he was groaning. This afternoon's try-outs were going to be even tougher than he'd expected.

Chapter Four

Daniel was on his way towards his first-period classroom when he heard someone call out his name.

It was Debi.

She was wearing a bright yellow tank top and a long, frothy skirt. She waved at him through the shifting crowd. 'Hey, are you heading to Mr Grant's social studies class?'

'Uh . . .' Daniel struggled to think over the pounding of his heart as she made her way over to him. Worse, his skin felt so hot under her gaze, he was sure he was blushing.

Then Debi raised her eyebrows, and Daniel

realised he still hadn't answered. *Come on, Packer.*
You know this one! 'Y-Y-Yes?' he said. 'I mean, *yes!*
I am.'

'Cool!' She smiled and fell into step beside
him, her long red hair bouncing around her
shoulders. 'I know almost no one here. It's great
that we have a class together.'

'Right,' Daniel said as they walked together
into the classroom. Just inside the doorway,
they stopped. Daniel gulped as her hair brushed
against his arm.

'Oh, and Riley signed me up for the book
society,' she said. 'Will you be joining that, too?'

'Umm . . .' Daniel tried to think. He really did.
But Debi was standing so close to him, he was
pretty sure his brain had just shorted out. Then
someone let out a low wolf whistle, and he jerked
out of his daze. The whole class was watching
them, including their teacher.

Mr Grant cleared his throat loudly. 'If

everyone is ready to settle down . . .?'

Daniel lurched into a seat. *Just please don't let me be blushing.* He could sense Debi taking the desk behind him, but he didn't dare look around. Instead, he kept his gaze focused on his teacher as if the formation of Pilgrim villages in early America was something he actually cared about.

Fat chance.

He was usually bored by History class, but today was just ridiculous. He'd never been so distracted in his life. His senses felt so acute, he thought he could hear pens scratching in classrooms all around him. It had to be his imagination, obviously, but he couldn't shut out the sound of the art teacher entertaining his class five rooms over:

'. . . so when the judge asked the thief why he'd stolen the Monet, he said, "Because I have nothing Toulouse!"'

Ouch. That pun was so bad, Daniel couldn't

stop himself from snickering.

'I beg your pardon?' Suddenly Mr Grant was looming directly over his desk. 'Do you find something about the Pilgrims' hats *amusing*, Mr Packer?'

'Uh . . .' Cringing, Daniel shook his head. 'No, sir.'

'No? Then why don't you explain to the entire class exactly what you *were* laughing at.'

As Daniel felt everyone in the room – including Debi – turn to stare at him, he sank lower in his seat. Under his desk, even his hands were burning with embarrassment. Amid the giggles around him, he forced the words out: 'It was nothing. Sir.'

'Nothing? Are you *sure*?' Mr Grant stayed there for a long moment, glowering down at Daniel.

When Mr Grant finally turned back to resume his lesson, Daniel let out a sigh of relief. Then he looked down at his hands . . . and froze.

Oh, no. They hadn't been burning with embarrassment after all. They'd been burning with *change*!

Panic thudded through him as he stared down at his hands. Long hair had sprouted across their backs. His nails were suddenly each at least half an inch long.

Daniel shoved his hands into his jeans pockets – but he couldn't hide the truth from himself any longer. He had to clamp his lips together to hold back a howl of panic. *It wasn't a dream after all. It was real! I really am a . . .*

He closed his eyes in misery.

. . . Weirdo!

Then his eyes flashed back open as he heard more laughing around him and he realised: he hadn't managed to completely muffle his howl after all. It had just come out as an odd, dog-like whine . . . and the whole class had heard it.

'Do you have something to add to our

discussion, Mr Packer?' Mr Grant asked coldly. 'Or are you entertaining the class by acting the clown?'

'No, sir,' Daniel mumbled. He stared down at his desk. *Be calm. Be calm.*

It was a lost cause. When something bumped against his shoe, he jumped so hard, his knees hit his desk.

'Sorry,' Debi whispered behind him. When Daniel turned to look at her, she made a rueful face and nodded her head towards the floor, where one of her pink gel pens had fallen next to Daniel's shoe. With Mr Grant droning on nearby, they couldn't speak, but she made a hopeful gesture with her hand: *Pass it to me, please?*

Daniel stared down at the pen, his chest suddenly tight. It should have been so easy to lean down and pick it up. It was the polite thing to do. The *normal* thing to do. But if Debi saw his hands right now . . .

He shuddered. *Then she'd know I'm a weirdo.*

There had to be another way.

Maybe if I just nudge it over to her with my foot . . .

He reached out with the toe of his shoe.

Just one little nudge . . .

The pen exploded in a shower of plastic and pink ink, which spattered everywhere. Gasps and shrieks erupted around him, but all Daniel could focus on was the massive pink stain spreading along Debi's skirt . . .

Slowly, painfully, he looked up to meet Debi's astonished gaze. He felt the room whirl around him. Other students were shouting and trying to wipe ink off their own clothes.

Before Daniel could say a word, their teacher was there, radiating fury.

'Mr Packer! What do you think you're doing?' Mr Grant's jaw worked as he stared at the ink-spattered devastation. Then he turned back to Daniel. 'And why are you sitting with your hands in your pockets now? Are you actually *trying* to be insolent as well as destructive?'

'No, sir,' Daniel mumbled. 'I'm sorry.' He slid further and further down in his seat. But the apology wasn't enough . . . and as his teacher's lecture thundered over him like a tidal wave, there was no way to hide from the truth.

This was *not* the birthday he'd been hoping for.

This is not *the birthday I was hoping for,* Justin thought.

It was finally time for try-outs, and he was in a huddle with the coach and the other guys trying out for Offense. They were all wearing full football gear, and in the privacy of their group, Coach obviously felt safe talking about *everything* he expected from them:

'You've got to use your wolfish senses to judge the plays, boys.'

What if I don't have any? Justin wanted to yell.

He bit back the words, trying to push down the panic in his chest.

It'll be OK, he told himself. *I've played with all these guys before in gym class.* Last semester, he'd even been one of the best players. *But of course, that was before the others changed . . .*

Still, there were some regular guys trying out for Defense and Special Teams on the squad. They wouldn't know that he *wasn't* a werewolf with extra-special abilities . . .

But the Beasts will.

He slid a glance at Kyle and the others as they listened to Coach's instructions. The Beasts might be loud, rude and over-the-top macho . . . but they weren't *total* idiots.

Then Ed Yancey and Chris Jordan head-butted each other so hard, they both fell over.

'Ha! Good one, dude!' they shouted at the same time.

OK, Justin thought. *Maybe they* are *idiots.*

As Coach straightened, clapping his hands for the try-outs to start, Justin took a deep breath. *I have to make this work . . . somehow.*

Gritting his teeth, he ran on to the field.

Within a few minutes, he was starting to relax. Werewolf or not, this was still football, the one thing he loved doing more than anything else in the world. As he made some great throws and catches, he felt himself getting into the swing of things.

Then Ed threw the ball to Justin . . . *hard.*

Ouch! Justin bit back a moan. Yeah, he'd caught it, but the force of the throw made it feel like he'd just taken a bowling ball to the chest. His hands stung, and his ribs felt like they'd shattered.

Get a grip, cub! he ordered himself.

That did it. Somehow, he found the energy to run. Carrying the ball close to his chest, he jumped over the first tackle. *Almost there . . .*

Then the second tackle hit hard and knocked Justin to the ground.

Am I dead?

A strong hand pulled Justin to his feet. It was Kyle. 'Good job faking being human,' he whispered, 'but you don't have to overdo it. Everyone's used to Pine Wood having super-strong players, even back when our dads played years ago.'

Justin nodded miserably. *I know.* His dad still kept his old football trophies in his study. He was waiting – *planning* – for Justin's trophies to join them.

'Forget about playing "human",' Kyle said. 'The locals are used to seeing our players running that little bit faster, hitting that little bit harder. Don't sweat it, OK?'

Justin tried to respond, but all that came out of his mouth was a series of wheezing gasps. He smiled weakly.

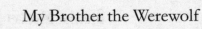

Don't sweat it? he thought, as he watched Kyle swagger away. *Like that's going to happen.*

Justin had spent the whole summer hoping to make it on to the football team . . . but now he wondered if he'd even make it out of the football try-outs alive.

I've gotta be the only player in the country more worried about my own team than our opponents, he thought, as he hunkered down for the next play.

At least the other schools didn't have werewolves on their teams!

'And . . . hup!' Kyle shouted, and Justin braced himself for more pain.

Daniel had never been so relieved to be on stage with his band. Sure, the school day had been excruciating, but now that it was over, all he had to think about was music: the one thing that always felt *right*. If they could just make their band a four-piece by finding one more guy to complete their hard rock sound, it really would be a birthday worth remembering.

Luckily the long hair had disappeared from the backs of his hands, now the only irritation was his stupid bangs. They kept flopping over his eyes, getting in his way every time he bent forwards to warm up on his guitar. As he shoved them back for what had to be the sixth time, he heard his friend Nathan clear his throat.

Daniel turned around. As always, Nathan looked the part: he had his army combats on, with his hair greased-up and half-dyed purple. He looked really cool – kinda like a skunk that had gotten caught in a paintball accident.

'Uh . . . Daniel?' Nathan pulled him aside, out of earshot of the other guys. The small auditorium was still empty; the auditions weren't due to begin for another fifteen minutes. 'What exactly is going on with your hair?'

Daniel stared at Nathan. 'You think there's

something wrong with *my* hair?'

Nathan nodded, his eyes wide.

This was serious. 'Give me a minute,' said Daniel. Setting down his guitar and grabbing his backpack, he ran to the closest bathroom.

The sight in the mirror made him groan. His hair had grown over an inch since this morning. It was out of control – and *not* in a good way!

Frantically, he scooped up handfuls of water from the sink to try to tame it – but it just stuck out more than ever.

I can't run auditions like this!

. . . *Wait.* Suddenly Daniel remembered the scissors in his backpack that he kept for Art class. Getting them out, he started cutting. Hair rained on to the floor. When he finished, he looked hopefully into the mirror.

Hmm. It was definitely shorter . . . but did it look OK?

A glance at his watch decided it for him. There was no more time to worry about his hair. Auditions were about to start!

He rushed out of the bathroom – and ran straight into someone walking past.

'Ooof!' Daniel stumbled back as pom-poms fluttered in front of his eyes like crazy pigeons.

When he looked up, his jaw dropped. Debi! *Why did it have to be Debi?* He'd bumped her so hard, she'd stumbled, too.

'I'm so sorry.' Cursing inwardly, he knelt down to pick up her pom-poms. *Why do I always have to act like an idiot around her?*

'That's OK. But, um, Daniel . . .' Debi frowned down at him. She'd changed into shorts and athletic shoes, and she bounced on her toes as she pointed at his hair. 'What happened to your –'

'My . . . what?' Daniel put a defensive hand to his chopped-short hair.

'Uh . . . never mind.' She put one hand to her

mouth, covering up her expression, but Daniel had a bad feeling that she might be hiding a grin. 'So, where are you headed?'

Daniel's shoulders relaxed, and he stood up. 'Auditions for my band. How about you?'

She pointed to the pom-poms in his hands. 'I'm on my way to cheerleading try-outs.'

'Oh. Right.' *Duh*. 'Then . . . I guess we'd better both wish each other luck.'

Debi smiled, leaning a little closer. 'Good luck, Daniel.'

Daniel's throat went completely dry. 'Good luck, Debi.'

He couldn't be late for the auditions. Taking a deep breath, he turned around.

'Daniel?' Her voice stopped him before he'd taken a single step. 'Aren't you forgetting something?'

'Huh?' Blinking, he turned back.

She pointed at his hands and grinned.

'My pom-poms. I need those back. Unless you planned to use them in your band?'

Oops. Heat crept across Daniel's face as he shoved the pom-poms at her. 'No! No. Sorry. Here.'

'Thank you.' Still smiling, she took them from him. Their fingers brushed for one long moment.

Then she walked away down the hall, cheerfully swishing the pom-poms in her hands.

For some reason, though, Daniel couldn't make himself move yet, auditions or not. He just stood there watching her as she bounced down the hall, opened a door . . .

. . . and was buried beneath an avalanche of mops, brooms and hand towels.

'Debi!' Daniel ran towards her. It was only as he reached her side that he realised he'd never run so fast before. He hadn't even known he *could* run that fast!

'I'm fine.' Shaking her head, Debi reached out of the avalanche to take his hand. As he helped her up, packets of hand towels slid off her shoulders to the floor. She started laughing, kicking away the mop that lay across her feet. 'I guess this room isn't the gym.'

'The gym?' Daniel stared at her as he helped her step free of the wreckage. 'That's on the other side of the building, near the pool.'

'But Mackenzie said . . .' Debi sighed. 'She gave me exact directions. I guess I must have gotten them confused somehow.'

'*Grrrr . . .*'

Too late, Daniel felt the growl build up in his throat.

Debi blinked, then glanced at his stomach. 'Feeling hungry?'

'I guess,' Daniel muttered, and forced the growl back down. 'Mackenzie used to live in the house you just moved into, and she's . . .'

He searched for a polite word to describe her. '. . . not very nice. Knowing Mackenzie, she did this because she doesn't want you at try-outs.'

'I guess there's a Charlotte Brown in every town,' Debi said, scowling at her shoes.

'"*A Charlotte Brown in every town*"? Hey, that rhymes!' Still feeling off-balance, Daniel laughed too hard. 'Maybe you should write some songs with me!'

Then his laughter died as Debi's mouth fell open and her gaze swung up to his. He saw the shocked look on her face – and he realised for the first time that he was still holding her hand.

Daniel dropped her hand, lurching backwards.

Does she think I just asked her out on some sort of song-writing date? That was not what I meant to say . . . was it?

His heart was pounding fast.

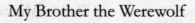

What if she says no? Would that mean he'd *never* have a chance with her?

Quick! Daniel cleared his throat. *Say something fast!* If he said something now before she could say 'no', then – *technically* – she wouldn't have rejected him. Then, maybe, sometime in the future, when he was feeling really brave – *and when I've gotten rid of all this freakiness* – he could finally ask her out properly.

'Daniel . . .' Debi began.

Don't let her say no!

'I'll take you to the gym!' he said. 'It's on the way to my auditions.'

'Oh. OK.' She nodded, looking down at her pom-poms.

Was that disappointment on her face? Or *relief*? Daniel was so confused, he couldn't even tell.

He knew one thing for sure, though. He was

going to be late to his own band's auditions. But, compared to the idea of getting turned down by Debi, he did not mind one bit.

Chapter Five

The first thing Justin saw as he came out of the changing room was Coach, pinning a list of names to the athletics board.

Justin froze. He wanted to see . . . But he also *didn't* want to see . . .

What if I didn't make it?

Get a grip, cub! He took a deep breath and slid to one side. *I'll just wait until everybody else is gone before I check.*

Waiting seemed to take forever, but finally the hallway emptied out. Feeling like a sneak-thief, Justin slipped across to the bulletin board. For just a moment, he closed his eyes, preparing himself. *Pleasepleaseplease* . . .

A heavy hand clapped against his back, making him jump. 'Yo, Packer!'

Justin spun around, his heartbeat racing. He found Kyle giving him a feral grin. 'Dude, do you really even need to check?!'

As Kyle's beefy arm swung through the air towards him, Justin tried not to cringe in anticipation.

He gritted his teeth behind his smile and accepted Kyle's bruising high-five. 'Seriously? I made the team?'

'Of course. But man, what was wrong with you today?' Kyle shook his head, trading glances with the other Beasts who had gathered behind him, crowding Justin against the board. 'Yeah, you did good out there, but it wasn't anywhere near as good as we were expecting. Have you got kennel cough or something?'

'Um . . .'

'He was probably thinking about some *girl*,' Chris Jordan suggested, grinning.

Justin felt his face flame. *How do they know about Riley?*

'Ha! Look at him. You're right!' Kyle bellowed with laughter. 'Don't blush too hard, Packer, you'll *turn*!'

The laughter from the other Beasts filled the hallway, and Justin wanted to melt into the floor with sheer embarrassment. *Still*, he thought, *it has to be better than if they knew the truth about me.*

Ed Yancey was still grinning as he reached into his pocket. 'Hey, you'll need this, dude.' He passed Justin a tube of hair gel. 'This'll keep things under control anytime you can't get to the barber's right away.'

'Um . . . right.' Justin pocketed the gel, only too aware that his hair hadn't grown a millimetre since last night. *I only* wish *I needed this.*

'So, what are the birthday plans?' Chris asked.

'Going howling up at Lycan Point? Getting your hair groomed?'

'Actually, I'm meeting my brother at the Meat & Greet,' Justin said. *I can't wait to hang out with someone who doesn't expect me to be a werewolf!*

'Hey, I'm feeling pretty hungry, too.' Kyle scratched his stomach. 'What do you think, dawgs? Shall we go along to help our new packmate celebrate?'

A chorus of rowdy agreement met his words, and Justin forced a smile. 'Great,' he said weakly.

Just no more high-fives, please . . .

Luckily, Kyle had to go back to his own locker before he'd be ready, and the other Beasts all wanted to go with him. They made plans to meet at the burger restaurant in twenty minutes . . . but for now Justin was free.

He had never been so happy to be on his own.

'*Oof.*' Finally, on his way out of the school, he could let out the groan that had been building all through try-outs.

Every muscle in his body ached. Every inch of his skin was sore. He felt like a punching bag that had just been through a long workout.

But I made it!

The thought made him grin even through the pain. He'd made it on to the team – Offense, no less – even without any special werewolf powers. He *rocked*!

He was feeling so pumped up from the triumph of it that, for once, he didn't even think about hiding when he saw Riley heading up the school steps towards him.

'Hey, Riley!' he called. He even waved.

Look at me! he thought. *I'm on the football team, and I'm talking to Riley, almost like a normal person!*

Then he saw her expression, and all his pride vanished, replaced by concern. Riley's eyebrows were furrowed, and she was biting her lip. He had never seen this look on her face before.

Could it be . . . *nerves?* Nah! She was a one-girl determination *machine!*

Justin started towards her, frowning. 'Are you OK?'

'Oh . . .' Riley brushed her hair out of her face and smiled unconvincingly, without meeting his eyes. 'I'm fine. How are you?'

'You don't look fine,' Justin said firmly. He stopped a step away from her, waiting for her to look at him. 'What's wrong?'

She shrugged, sighing. 'Nothing. How were the try-outs?'

Justin grinned, barely restraining himself from doing a victory strut. 'I'm officially Pine Wood Junior High's new running back.'

'That's great, Justin. You really deserve it.' But her smile faded quickly. 'Now I'm on my way to try-outs of my own.'

'Try-outs? Which – ? Hey!' Before Justin could finish his question, he heard a sharp and all-too-familiar yap close by.

Oh, no . . .

It was his neighbour's Chihuahua dog, Poochy! He must have gotten loose again. Tiny and fluffy, Poochy was the cutest furball that had ever walked on four paws, but his brain was as big as a pea – and he had been absolutely fixated on Justin for years.

'I've gotta go!' Justin turned to run down the rest of the steps. But he had pushed his aching body too far. His leg muscles, which had carried him all through that brutal training session, finally gave out completely.

His foot skidded across the edge of the step. He began to fall.

Poochy landed on top of him with a shrill yap of joy and went to town, licking his face.

As Justin lay helplessly pinned on the wide stone steps, feeling Poochy cover his face with his sloppy tongue, he heard Riley burst into giggles.

'Awwww,' she said. 'Isn't he sweet?'

'Adorable,' Justin agreed through gritted teeth. 'Do you think you could get him off me? Please?'

Riley scooped Poochy up into her arms and cooed over him, still giggling. 'Who's a big scary puppydog? Is that you? Yes it is! You trapped that big brave running back, didn't you?'

Justin had to fight back a groan as he picked himself up.

I can't believe I just got beaten up by a tiny dog . . . and in front of Riley, too!

Daniel was finally beginning to relax as he led Debi to the gym. Ever since the whole songwriting-date-offer debacle, everything had actually been going OK. He'd gotten Debi to start telling him about her friends back at Franklin Grove, and the stories she told him were really funny.

As he drank in the sound of her laughter, he

realised that Debi wasn't just pretty and fun – she was genuinely nice. And from the way she kept sliding glances up at him, she might not think he was too bad, either. Maybe he really *did* have a chance!

Their gazes met as they walked, and Debi glanced down, fiddling with her silver necklace. Daniel found himself remembering something he'd read a while ago.

When a girl played with her jewellery, that was supposed to be a sign that she liked you, wasn't it?

'Ah-choo!' A sudden sneeze took him by surprise. He covered his mouth. Too late, he saw the back of his hand.

Oh, no. It's back! His hands were covered with hair again. *Please don't let Debi have seen that!* He shoved his hands hastily back in his pockets, fighting the urge to sneeze again. A strange buzzing started in his head. *What is wrong with me?*

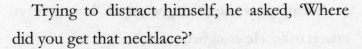

Trying to distract himself, he asked, 'Where did you get that necklace?'

Debi let it go, looking a little embarrassed. 'It was my grandma's. Sorry, I'm always playing with it. I don't even realise I'm doing it.'

'That's OK.' He smiled, trying to think through the dizzying buzzing sensation in his head. Unfortunately, it was spreading out to fill his whole body. 'It's pretty.'

'Do you think?' She scooped up the pendant and held it out until it nearly touched his nose. 'Here, take a closer look.'

As the glint of silver shone into his eyes, Daniel turned his head and sneezed again. 'Sorry!' He backed away hastily – and felt the buzzing sensation subside.

Wait a minute . . . Is the necklace doing this to me? Was it even possible to be allergic to silver? *How could that happen? Don't let her figure out what a freak you are,* he told himself.

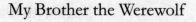

As casually as he could, he asked, 'Do you ever take it off?' He coughed.

She glanced up from wiping off the pendant, looking startled. 'Never,' she said. Her eyes widened. 'Why? Don't you like it?'

'Uh . . .' Daniel tried to think of a polite answer, but it was all he could do just to stop himself from sneezing on to it again. He jerked his chin towards the double doors ahead of them, keeping his hands in his pockets. 'Here's the gym.'

'Right.' Debi sighed, letting go of the necklace. 'Thanks for getting me here.'

Daniel smiled awkwardly, hating the distant look on her face. *Yup. I definitely hurt her feelings.*

'Good luck,' he said.

'You, too,' she said quietly.

Hunching his shoulders, Daniel turned to walk away.

'Wait. Daniel!' she called, when he was only three steps away.

'Yeah?' He turned around so quickly, he nearly knocked against the lockers.

'I almost forgot!' Flashing a hilariously exaggerated rockstar grimace, Debi held up her hands to make the 'rock out' hand-signal. 'For luck!'

Laughing, Daniel started to pull his own hands out to return the gesture . . . then froze. *I can't let her see my hands!* His laughter died in his throat. *I'm going to look like such a jerk . . .* There had to be something he could say or do to make this better . . . but his mind had gone completely blank. He just nodded.

Still holding her own hands up in the signal, Debi looked down to Daniel's hands, still pointedly stuck in his pockets. Her smile disappeared. For a moment, real hurt flashed across her face. Then she turned and slipped through the double doors without another word.

'Gaaaaaaah!' Daniel moaned and knocked his

head against the closest locker.

So much for having a chance. Doofus!

He pulled his hands out of his pocket and groaned as he saw the long, curving nails at the end of his fingers.

What the heck was up with him?

Chapter Six

Daniel couldn't believe it: he was going to be epically late for his own band's auditions. He'd had to spend the last ten minutes hiding in an empty classroom, just waiting for the freakishness to stop. *Hard to hide furry hands when you're playing guitar!*

As the last hair finally disappeared, he shuddered. *Please don't let it happen again . . .* As he headed out the door, he sent a quick text to Justin:

Got delayed. I'll be late to Meat & Greet.

There wasn't time to make up any excuses. The small auditorium was already crowded with hopefuls. Guys filled the seats, from Goths to preps, jocks to nerds. The one thing they had in common was the 'rock out' sign they made as Daniel walked down the main aisle

Just like Debi. Wincing at the reminder, Daniel made the sign back at them, then hurried down the aisle to jump on stage with his bandmates.

Nathan traded a look with Otto, who was sitting behind the drums. Under his breath, so the waiting singers couldn't hear, Nathan hissed: 'Where have you been for the last half-hour? We're not famous enough to leave the audience waiting, man!'

'Ah . . . sorry about that.' Daniel took a deep breath. 'I just –'

'And what is *up* with your hair? Last time I saw you, it was super-long. Now it's all jagged!'

'Don't ask.' Daniel scooped up his guitar and slung the strap across his shoulder. As he plucked the strings, checking the tuning, he felt himself begin to relax. *I just wish I could get my life back in tune.*

But he didn't have time to think about that now. 'Come on,' he said, and looked out at the crowd of guys waiting for them. 'Let's get these auditions started!'

Justin was sitting in a booth at the Meat & Greet, surrounded by the Beasts, when his phone chimed. He read the message from Daniel and sighed.

Great, he thought. *Now I'll have to wait even longer to go home and lie down.*

With every inch of his body aching, it was hard to summon up enthusiasm, even as the Beasts joked and roughhoused around him. He just smiled faintly and tried to avoid any more high-fives.

The waitress had to speak twice before the Beasts paid attention. 'Can I take your orders?'

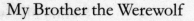

'Absolutely!' Kyle grinned and leaned forwards. 'Burger. *Very* rare. Got it?'

She raised her eyebrows, looking amused. 'I think we can probably handle that. And the rest of you?'

From first to last, they all copied Kyle's order until . . .

'A veggie burger please,' Justin said.

'Yeah, right!' Ed Yancey bellowed with laughter as he pounded Justin painfully on the back. 'Good one, man. High five!'

Do I have to? 'Maybe later,' Justin muttered. He kept his hands tightly buried in his pockets.

'So that'll be another burger, extra rare?' the waitress asked, looking bored now.

Justin felt all the Beasts' eyes on him. 'Uh . . . yeah, I guess.'

'Whatever.' Shaking her head in frustration, she stomped off to the next booth.

Kyle was now looking at Justin with a frown

on his face. 'You know, Packer, sometimes I can't work you out.'

'Who, me?' Justin forced himself to grin. 'No mysteries here, dude.'

'What about taking out those Tigers next week?' Chris put in. 'No way can we lose to them in our first game.'

Snarls of agreement filled the booth. The Tigers were from Grover Middle School, just one town over. They had been Pine Wood's biggest rivals for as long as anyone could remember.

'We're counting on you, Packer.' Kyle didn't slap Justin on the back this time, but his eyes bored into him, as predatory as any alpha wolf's gaze. 'We're going to teach those losers a lesson.'

'No problem,' Justin drawled. 'I'll be ready.'

Inside, though, he was cringing. He had at least a month to wait until he turned full wolf. *What am I going to do?*

He'd shut down his dad last night, but today

he was definitely going after some answers.
There had to be something he could do to speed
up the transformation process! Maybe eating rare
burgers would actually help get his body into the
wolf spirit?

But when the waitress reappeared, holding a
tray full of their orders, he almost dry-heaved.

*Rare? Those burgers don't look like they've ever even
seen a grill!*

As she set down his burger in front of him,
he tried not to gag. Red goo ran down the side
of the soft-looking meat. If Justin hadn't been
packed into the booth between Ed and Kyle, he
would have made a run for it.

There was no way out, though, with all of
the Beasts tearing happily into their own burgers
around him.

'Awesome!' Ed declared. His mouth was
so full, the word came out sounding more like:
'*Aweshum!*'

'Yeah,' Justin muttered. Staring at his burger, he swallowed hard. 'Just . . . awesome.'

'Hey, how come you're not eating?' Chris asked.

All the Beasts stopped to look. Justin's head went completely blank.

If he tried to eat it, he'd throw up. But after the try-out he'd just been through, his stomach felt so hollow it hurt. It growled ominously – and the sound made the Beasts around him snicker.

That's it. Pretend it was on purpose!

'Grrrrr,' Justin said. 'Sorry about that. I just can't help growling, I'm so hungry . . . for my burger! My . . . rare . . . burger . . .'

The Beasts broke into enormous grins.

'*Grr!*' They all growled along. '*Grrrrrrr!*'

Grinning desperately, Justin started picking at his fries. *I wonder how much trouble I'd get into with that waitress if I 'accidentally' knocked my plate off the table . . .*

Daniel couldn't believe how many guys had shown up for the audition . . . and how few of them had talent! It took a full hour after the auditions had started before the crowd of wannabes finally thinned down.

Daniel huddled on stage with his bandmates, comparing notes on the last auditionee they'd seen. Milo had been the best so far, they all agreed, but that really wasn't saying much. Not one of the singers they'd heard so far had the *feel* of a real rock star – and Milo's singing was only for himself. He paid *no* attention to the band around him.

Daniel sighed as he straightened from the huddle. 'Next!' he called.

As he turned around, someone stepped up to the stage . . . and tripped on the final step, just barely catching herself.

'Wait a minute . . .' Daniel muttered.

For the first time that afternoon, the singer wasn't a guy. She was a girl. A really *familiar* girl.

'Riley, what are you doing here?' Daniel said. 'Choral try-outs are in the main auditorium. Well, they were. I think you missed –'

'I know. I've just come from there. I am the *head* of the choral society, you know?' Riley rolled her eyes, looking as preppy as ever in her button-up white shirt and knee-length skirt. 'And now I'm here to audition for *In Sheep's Clothing.*'

'Good one,' Daniel let out a snort of laughter as his bandmates snickered behind him.

'You didn't get hard rock mixed up with honors society, did you?' Nathan said.

'Or prep club,' Otto muttered, not nearly quietly enough.

Daniel cleared his throat as he saw Riley flush. Aiming a glare at his bandmates, he tried to think of a polite approach. 'Um, the guys are just kidding, but . . . this isn't exactly . . . your thing, is it?'

Riley glared at him, setting her hands on her hips. 'You haven't heard me sing yet, Daniel Packer.'

Otto rolled his eyes. 'Do we really need to?'

Daniel winced. Riley might not be what they were looking for . . . but she didn't deserve to be humiliated, either. 'Come on, dude. She's got the nerve to audition. That's pretty rock 'n' roll.'

Nathan shrugged. 'She can't suck any more than some of the others.'

Otto shook his head. 'OK . . .'

'If you're really sure, Riley?' Daniel added gently.

He'd known Riley ever since they were little kids. The last thing he wanted was to see her embarrass herself in front of the other guys.

Riley rolled her eyes at him but didn't bother to reply. Instead, she looked past him to his bandmates. 'Do you guys know "Back in Black"?'

Huh, Daniel thought. *Who knew Riley listened to AC/DC?*

Nathan broke into a grin. 'I love that song.'

Otto nodded, settling behind the drum set. 'This girl's got taste.'

The band started playing and as Riley began to sing Daniel's mouth dropped open in shock. Her voice belted through the auditorium, strong and vibrant. All her clumsiness seemed to have disappeared as she strode around the stage, alternately prowling and leaping to the beat of the music. Every inch of her was focused on the auditorium, playing to an audience that wasn't even there.

She didn't just know her classics; Riley was a born performer! And with her belting vocal power and energy, the whole band raised their game. They'd never played so well before.

All except Daniel. He found himself hitting

wrong chord after wrong chord. Cursing his own clumsiness, he glanced down at his fingers – and choked back a groan.

His nails were insanely long. It made fingering impossible.

And his nails weren't the only thing that had changed.

'Hold up!' Otto lifted one hand. In the sudden silence, Riley's voice was the last sound to fade away, a beat behind the rest.

Otto was staring at Daniel. 'What's up with you? I've never heard you make so many mistakes.'

'Uh . . .'

'Is something wrong with your nails?' Riley asked. She started towards him, frowning. 'And your hands are really *hairy*. Have they always –'

'I'm fine!' Daniel shoved his hands in his pockets.

Why does Riley have to have such sharp eyes? His face was tingling with embarrassment, but he managed to nod at her like he was still in charge.

'Thank you, Riley. That was –'

'No really,' she said, still staring at his hands. 'What is up with your hands? I've never noticed –'

'Riley,' he said, cutting her off by nodding to the microphone she was holding. 'I think we've heard enough.'

'OK.' Suddenly, she seemed to morph, as if she was transforming in front of him from confident rock chick back to awkward, preppy girl. Her shoulders slumped with obvious disappointment, but she gave a polite smile anyway. 'Thanks for letting me try out, guys.'

She didn't trip on her way down the stairs. But Daniel felt his own balance wavering as he watched her go.

The band waited in silence until the big doors of the auditorium closed behind her. Then Nathan let out a low whistle. 'I think we've found our lead singer.'

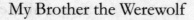

'I don't know, man,' Otto said. 'I mean, she's a great singer, and she really knows her rock, but . . . she's a . . . you know . . .' Otto looked at the others and raised his eyebrows. 'She's a . . . *girl*.'

'She out-rocked every guy we saw,' Nathan said.

Otto groaned. 'If we have some preppy, girly-girl singer, we'll just end up playing sappy ballads all the time.'

Daniel doubted that. The Riley he'd just seen on stage had aced it like she did every exam.

'Choose Milo,' Otto said firmly.

But as much as the injustice burned, he had to be practical. Riley was the only one who'd noticed the change in his hands. If they let her into the band, he'd never keep his secret safe. She absolutely deserved the spot. But . . .

Daniel hated himself for what he was about to say.

'I agree with Otto,' he mumbled, the lie

burning in his throat. Riley wasn't just a better singer than Milo, she had a natural feel for rock that Milo would never be able to match. *If only she wasn't so observant!*

'Well, I don't agree . . .' Nathan groaned, tugging at his purple and black hair in frustration. 'Let's hold call-backs for both of them, OK? We'll do one final audition to decide who *really* belongs in the band.'

'Okaaaay,' said Otto.

'Sure,' Daniel muttered. 'OK.'

Scratching at the back of one itchy hand – *ouch!* – he just hoped that Milo upped his game between now and then . . . for Daniel's sake. Having Riley in the band was a risk he wasn't willing to take.

Justin let out a sigh of relief as he saw his brother walk through the doors of the Meat & Greet.

As the Beasts shifted to make room, Justin

signalled for the waitress. 'Your usual, Bro?'

He was already relaxing as the waitress started towards them. Everything about this birthday might be different from what he'd imagined beforehand, but at least some things never changed. Daniel had eaten a chicken burger on his birthday every year that Justin could remember. It was a family tradition.

'Actually . . .' As Daniel slid into the booth beside Justin, he glanced across the table, and his eyes lit up. 'You know what? Those rare beef burgers look great.'

'Are you serious?' Justin stared at his brother. 'Dude, you don't even *like* red meat.'

Daniel gave a half-smile, but his eyes were shadowed. 'I'm thirteen today, and things have changed.'

Justin frowned, trying to read his twin's expression. 'You OK?'

'Wait a minute.' Ed was frowning. 'It's your birthday today, too, just like Justin?' He shook his head, a big grin spreading across his face. '*Whoa*. What are the chances of that!'

'Yeah,' Justin muttered. *Ever heard of twins before, Ed?*

Then he cringed as he saw Ed swinging his meaty hand back to high-five Daniel. 'Wait —'

But it was too late. To Justin's shock, Daniel only smiled as he returned the high-five. Obviously, Justin's rock-star brother was putting on a brave face so he wouldn't embarrass his twin in front of the Beasts.

I owe him big, Justin thought — then winced as he saw Ed turning to give *him* another high-five, too.

'Sorry, dude.' He held up his burger. 'But my hands are full.'

'How long do you need to eat one burger,

dawg?' Chris said. 'I'm on my third already!'

'It's gotta be ice-cold by now,' Ed added.

'Just the way I like it.' Justin forced a cocky grin.

I just hope I don't have to take a bite to prove it!

Daniel couldn't wait for his burger to arrive. Just the sight of all the others on the table was making him salivate. If Justin didn't eat his own burger soon, Daniel might just have to steal it.

He'd never before had a craving like this – especially not for red meat. He couldn't wait.

But *what* was wrong with Justin? As Daniel forced his gaze away from the burger, he finally took in the exhaustion on his twin's face. Justin looked like he'd run a marathon, then missed the bus home.

Come to think of it, that line could be the basis of a pretty good song lyric. *I'd better write that down before I forget it – or lose control and grab someone else's burger!*

Daniel reached into Justin's bag, searching for a pen. Instead, his hands closed around a small tube. Frowning, he pulled it out.

'Hair gel?' He blinked at the tube. 'Since when do you wear hair gel?'

'Um . . .' Justin shifted, while the Beasts nudged each other and snickered. 'It's a new kind,' Justin finally muttered. 'It stops your hair from growing too fast.'

Suddenly, Daniel couldn't have cared less about song lyrics. 'Can I borrow it?'

'Since when do *you* wear hair gel?' Justin asked.

'Ah . . .' Daniel looked into his brother's confused expression and felt his stomach twist. If it hadn't been for the Beasts sitting all around them, he might have lost control and told him everything. They were twins. They were supposed to share stuff. And maybe, if this was happening to Daniel, it might just be happening to Justin, too.

As Kyle and Ed started swapping plans for the upcoming football game, Daniel lowered his voice and spoke directly into Justin's ear. 'Did anything . . . weird happen to you today?'

Justin's face went as pale as chalk. 'No! Why? Do you think I've changed?'

Daniel blinked. 'No. Why? Do you think *I've* changed?'

'Why would you have changed?'

'Why would *you*?'

The waitress broke into their conversation, sounding annoyed. '*Another* rare beef burger?'

'Mine!' Daniel said. He was stuffing the burger into his mouth before his plate had even reached the table. It was the most delicious thing he'd ever tasted . . . but from the expression on Justin's face, his twin had never been more confused by him.

Daniel only wished he didn't feel the same way.

Chapter Seven

That night, Justin met his twin's eyes over the flickering candles of their birthday cake and grinned. This really had been the weirdest birthday ever . . . but right now, together, they were about to perform one of their most important birthday traditions, and it felt just right.

The twins blew out their candles.

'Hey!' Justin had to skip backwards. One of the candles Daniel had blown out lifted clean out of the icing and flew past him. 'Watch it, dude!'

'Sorry,' Daniel mumbled.

Their dad cleared his throat. *Uh-oh*, Justin

thought. *Lecture incoming.* He shared a look with his brother.

Their dad, however, was beaming. 'Your mother and I have never been more proud of you. You may be entering into a new phase of your life . . . *changing* . . . but you are becoming the men you were meant to be. I cannot wait to share this . . . *new* part of your life with you.'

Justin tried not to squirm. Yet again, Dad was looking only at him. Daniel's grin seemed to fade as he took in the shared bond between Justin and their dad, made painfully obvious by Mr Packer's proud expression.

I just wish there was some way to include Daniel, Justin thought miserably. *But Dad's right. What's the point in telling him something that will only make him feel more left out?*

Their mom cleared her throat. 'What would you boys say to opening presents *before* you eat your cake this year?'

117

At that, the moment of tension was broken. 'Yessss!' the twins yelled.

Mom and Dad went to the cabinet at the side of the room, opening the door with a theatrical flourish. A stack of wrapped presents sat inside. 'Ta-da!'

Dad scooped off a large package and tossed it across the room to Justin. 'Catch!'

Justin tore the wrapping paper off and tried not to shout with joy. A pair of gleaming new football boots rested inside the box, with 'PACKER' stitched across their sides. 'These are awesome!'

'Ready to kick some Tiger butt in those?' Dad asked.

'Oh, yeah!' Justin pulled off his shoes and started lacing on the boots right then and there. 'No one will stand a chance against me in these!'

'And for you, Daniel,' said Mom, 'a real surprise . . .'

Justin looked up just in time to see Mom hand a large parcel to his twin, smiling.

No prizes for guessing what that is! Justin thought. Daniel had been begging for a new guitar for months now.

Still, Daniel's mouth dropped open in wonder as he peeled back the wrapping paper to reveal the sleek red guitar underneath.

'You really got it for me!'

Justin rolled his eyes. 'Duh! How many times did you drag me in to visit that guitar store? Like you were ever going to get anything else!'

'Shh,' Mom said gently. She reached out to ruffle Daniel's hair. 'Of course we got it for you. You'll need a really good guitar for your band, won't you?'

'This is just . . .' Daniel shook his head, still staring down at the guitar in his lap as Mom started cutting slices of their birthday cake. He stroked gently down one of the strings then looked up at their dad, his eyes shining. 'Is this what you and Justin were talking about in the garden last night?'

Justin's face burned. 'Err, no . . .' he muttered quietly . . .

. . . just as Dad said, 'Yup! You guessed it.'

Oops. Justin gulped as Daniel looked between the two of them. 'The band!' Justin said hastily, as he took a plate of cake and ice cream. 'Tell us about the auditions.'

'Oh . . .' Daniel frowned. 'They went OK, I guess. Hey, guess who auditioned?

'Who?'

'Riley,' said Daniel. 'Isn't that weird?'

'*Riley?*' Justin spat his birthday cake back on to his plate. 'She really did it? Dude! You have to let her in the band!'

'Well . . .' Daniel looked even more uncomfortable than ever. 'The thing is . . . I mean, she did a good job, but –'

'No buts,' Justin said, and pointed his fork at Daniel commandingly. 'Let her in. She'll be awesome. And if your band needs any help with anything, I'll be happy to be your streetie!'

Daniel laughed. 'You mean, *roadie?*'

'Whatever,' Justin shrugged. 'You name it, I'll do it.'

'You will?' Daniel's eyes narrowed. The phone rang out in the hallway, but he didn't look around. 'You never made that offer before.'

'So?' Justin could feel his cheeks flaming. Had he just been too obvious? He tried to seem casual as he speared another bite of cake. 'I'm just trying to be supportive,' he said through his mouthful.

'Hmm.' Daniel looked dangerously thoughtful, even as he scooped a bite of ice cream. 'But you waited until I said Riley –'

'Oh, Daniel,' their mother sang, as she stood in the doorway, holding the phone and smirking. 'The phone's for you, hon.'

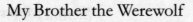

Daniel walked towards her with his hand out for the phone.

'It's Debi,' Mom said with a grin.

'What?!' Daniel's mouth dropped open, revealing a big chunk of still-uneaten ice cream inside.

Wait a minute. Justin blinked and leaned forwards. *Did his teeth just grow?*

Before he could get another look, Daniel had grabbed the phone from Mom and hurried out of the room.

Justin stared after him, dazed. *I've never seen him act so freaky before. And that thing with his teeth . . . and the burger . . . the rare burger . . . and . . . and . . .*

He swallowed hard, feeling the ice cream curdle in his stomach. If he didn't know better, he might actually think that Daniel . . .

No. He couldn't be . . . Could he?

122

As Daniel ran to his room for privacy, his mind was a panicked jumble. Had Mom noticed his hairy hands when he'd taken the phone from her? And why was Debi calling anyway? How had she even gotten his number?

And most of all: what was he going to say!?

He closed his bedroom door behind him and stared at the phone in his hand as if it were a poisonous snake. His teeth felt too big in his mouth. His tongue felt as tangled as his thoughts.

Still, he stiffened his shoulders. *You can't put it off forever.* Slowly, he raised the phone to his ear, feeling his long nails scrape against the sides of the plastic.

'Hello?' His voice came out as a low, raspy growl.

'Daniel?' Debi sounded startled. 'Are you OK? You sound a little –'

'I'm fine!' Wincing, Daniel put on a high-pitched voice to cover his gruffness. 'How are you?' he asked, in a near-falsetto.

I think I actually squeaked! But it wasn't enough. Even as he spoke, he felt the telltale itching across his body and the tingling in his teeth. *Please don't change now. Please!*

'Oh, I'm fine!' Debi said brightly. 'I was just calling to thank you for helping me get to the try-outs this afternoon.'

'Try-outs?' Daniel piped desperately, as his nails turned into claws. 'Oh, right! Try-outs. Cheerleading.' Fur spread across Daniel's arms as he watched in horror. Frantically, he tried to remember what he was supposed to be talking about. 'Um. How did they go?'

'Pretty well. I think I made the team.'

Now Daniel's face was tingling, too. 'That's great,' he said desperately. 'Well . . . Thanks for letting me know, but –'

'Soooo . . .' She drew out the word. 'Can I give you a manicure?'

'*What?*' Daniel stared at the phone in his hands. *How does she know what's going on with my hands . . . What* is *going on with my hands?*

'As a thank you,' she said. 'I'm pretty good at them, if I do say so myself.' She laughed, but it sounded nervous.

'Um . . .' Daniel could barely breathe as he felt the fur spread across his face. 'I'm not sure . . .' He walked to the mirror.

'Don't worry,' she said. 'Manicures can be manly, if that's what you're worried about.'

His reflection looked nothing like him. His face was covered in brown fur. His ears had grown tall. His nose was long, and when he opened his mouth to look at his teeth he saw they were fierce and sharp.

Debbie was still talking. 'I won't put any coloured polish on, I promise!'

Daniel tried to laugh. It came out more like a groan.

He wasn't a human any more; he was . . .

. . . a wolf.

When she spoke again, she sounded subdued. 'It's OK if you don't want to. I just noticed that your nails were pretty long, and I thought you might like it.'

Like it? She was offering to hold hands with him! He would have *loved* that idea . . . if it wasn't for the fact that he had turned into a wolf before his own eyes!

'I've gotta go,' he mumbled into the phone, as his nails lengthened and curved around it. He could feel the fur on his face tickling against the mouthpiece.

'OK,' she said. 'Well, maybe I'll see –'

'Bye.' He stabbed the 'off' button with one claw-like nail before she could even answer. Sinking down to the floor, he curled himself into a ball.

I want the last twenty-four hours to have never happened.

A knock sounded on the door behind him.

'Go away!' Daniel growled. Then he pushed his face harder against his knees. He could feel that his face was covered in fur like it was last night. He felt the howl threatening to break loose.

'Daniel?' Justin's voice was quiet but full of sympathy. 'I think I know what's going on. It's OK, though – really, it is. If you just let me in –'

'No!' Daniel lifted his head to yell his answer. 'Don't . . .'

But it was too late. The door was already opening behind him.

All that Justin could see when he stepped into the bedroom was his brother's back. Daniel was sitting on the floor with his arms wrapped around his legs and his face to the wall. He didn't even turn when Justin stepped inside and closed the door.

Remember what Mom always says, Justin told himself. *Be sensitive! Because I'm pretty sure he's a mess right now.*

'So,' he said. 'You like Debi, huh?'

Daniel groaned and buried his face against his knees.

Justin winced. *So much for sensitivity.*

Sighing, he hunkered down a few feet behind Daniel, so he wouldn't be talking down to his brother. 'Did something happen when you talked to her?' he asked. 'You can tell me, it's OK –'

'Trust me . . .' Daniel's voice came out as a rasping growl. 'It's *not* OK. And neither am I. So I need you to leave me alone right now!'

Justin put one hand on his brother's hunched shoulder. 'Look, I know what's going on. You don't need to hide it from me. You're thirteen now. It's natural –'

Daniel shook off his hand without looking up.

'There is nothing *natural* about what's happening to me!'

Oh, man. Justin stared at the back of his brother's head. Daniel's hair was so long now, it reached the collar of his shirt. *How did we not see this coming?*

At least now Justin knew why nothing had happened to him last night. He wasn't the werewolf in his family after all!

So, it hadn't been an act earlier at the Meat & Greet – Ed's high-five really hadn't hurt Daniel . . . because Daniel had werewolf strength. But he also obviously had no idea what was going on, and that was partly Justin's fault.

I have to make this right, Justin thought, taking a deep breath. He'd deal with the rest of it – and what it meant for him – later. Right now, he owed his brother a serious explanation.

'Dude,' he said. 'Will you just turn around?'

'No,' Daniel snarled. His shoulders hunched

tighter than ever.

'You don't have to worry about shocking me,' Justin said gently. 'I mean it – I really *do* know what's going on. No matter what, you know you'll always be my twin. Whatever's happened to you, I'm here. Always.'

For a long moment, nothing happened. Then Daniel let out a shuddering sigh. 'OK, Bro,' he whispered. 'You asked for it.'

Slowly, he turned around . . . and Justin looked into the face of his brother, the werewolf.

Daniel forced himself to hold still and let Justin see the full freakish effect. Sure, Justin wasn't looking shocked yet, but he had to be feeling completely horrified and disgusted. Maybe he didn't want to hurt Daniel's feelings by showing it, or maybe he was paralysed with disgust, but . . .

Wait a minute. Was Justin smiling? No – he was laughing!

Daniel's mouth dropped open. 'This is *not* funny!'

'Actually, it is.' Justin shook his head, still laughing. 'If you only knew –'

'Trust me, I know!' Daniel said, through gritted teeth. 'Look at my face! I'm a freak!' Then his stomach dropped, and he scooted back on the carpeted floor. 'Wait a minute. Is that why you're laughing?'

'No!' Justin put out one hand to stop him. 'It's just . . . well, this explains a *lot*.'

'It does?' Daniel frowned. *What does he mean by that?* 'Why are you taking this so well? You should be disgusted. Or scared.'

'Well, I'm not,' Justin said. 'And I'll tell you everything, I promise. But first, we really need to get Dad up here.'

'No!' Daniel jerked upright, panic surging through him. 'I don't want Dad to see me like this!'

But Justin was already opening the door. 'Dad!' he called.

'Noooooooo!' Daniel yelled. Horrified, he heard it turn into a howl. Dad had never been as proud of him as he was of Justin. And when he saw what had happened to Daniel now he'd . . .

Daniel couldn't even breathe as his dad stepped through the doorway, followed by his mom. Dad's eyes went straight to Daniel's furry face. His own face turned pale. Behind Dad, Mom put one hand to her mouth. Her eyes were wide and shocked.

Now they both know I'm a freak, Daniel told himself, closing his eyes.

When he opened them again, though, his parents were smiling.

Smiling? Daniel felt as dizzy as if the room had just tilted off-balance. *What is* wrong *with this family?*

'Well,' Dad said. 'This explains everything.'

Why do people keep saying that?!

Mom shook her head, her smile turning rueful. 'Really, we should have guessed it earlier.'

They always *thought I was a freak?*

Daniel put his head in his hands, hearing his parents kneel down on either side of him.

Dad's voice was firm. 'Daniel, I know you must be feeling pretty confused right now, but you can take it from me: this is normal.'

Daniel let out a bark of laughter that hurt his throat. He felt the fur on his face brush against his hands, and his stomach clenched. 'How can *this* be "normal"?'

Dad let out a long breath that ruffled Daniel's hair. 'It's my fault. I assumed that Justin would be the one to turn. He showed all the characteristics, ever since the two of you were little kids.'

'That's why he was the one we told,' Mom added. She rubbed her hand in a comforting circle on his back, the way she had done ever since he was a baby. 'We were wrong, and I'm *so* sorry, sweetheart.'

Behind his hands, Daniel shook his head. His throat felt so choked up, his voice came out in a rasp. 'You told Justin and not me?'

'It was meant for your own good,' Dad said. 'But now I wish we *had* told you. This must have been a really hard day for you, huh?'

Daniel couldn't help but laugh. 'You could say that,' he mumbled.

'I'm sorry, Daniel.' Dad squeezed his shoulder. 'But I want you to know, your whole family is here for you.'

'We all love you,' Mom said firmly, 'and we are so proud of you.'

Daniel had to squeeze his eyes shut to hold back the burning. 'How could you be proud of me right now?'

There was a moment of silence. Then Dad said, 'Drop your hands, and look me in the eye.'

Daniel hunched his shoulders, pressing his hands harder against his furry face. 'No.'

'Daniel.' His dad's voice was stern.

Reluctantly, Daniel let his hands fall away from his face. He looked up . . . and his breath caught in his throat.

Staring back at him were eyes he'd recognise anywhere. His dad's eyes. But they were surrounded by thick tufts of dark brown hair, long ears, a muzzle and a long face. *Just like mine.*

'You're . . . you . . . too?' he whispered.

'I'm a wolf,' Dad said.

Daniel's head was spinning again as he tried to put together all the pieces. How much had his family been hiding from him over the years? 'And Mom?'

'No,' Mom said. Her face was unchanged, her expression calm. 'I'm a "were" – a human.'

Daniel took a minute to let that sink in. Then

a thousand other questions flooded him. He opened his mouth to speak.

'Hang on.' Dad held up one furry hand to silence him, claws glinting in the light from the overhead lamp. 'I know you must have lots of questions, but now isn't the time to get into it all. You've had a long day, and you need your sleep. Tomorrow night, you and I will go on the traditional father–cub camping trip . . . *Then,* I will teach you the ways of the wolf.'

The ways of the wolf. Dad's last words rang in Daniel's head, echoing again and again as he watched his parents walk out of the room. When he was finally able to close his mouth, he turned and found Justin looking at him with a look of surprise.

'What a family, huh?' Justin said. 'I'm glad it's not just me dealing with this any more.'

Daniel sighed. It was all too much to take in right now.

But . . . Suddenly, he frowned, remembering that afternoon at the Meat & Greet – and how Justin had gone so blatantly out of his way to avoid high-fiving the other football players there. Now that he came to think of it, that guy had given a pretty strong high-five. It hadn't hurt Daniel, but . . .

'Are the other football players werewolves, too?' he asked.

'Not the whole team,' Justin said. 'Just the ones who play Offense. The Beasts.'

'But you just got put on Offense, didn't you?' Daniel asked. Then he sucked in a breath. 'Wait a minute. Dad thought you were going to be the werewolf in the family. Did *they* think so, too?'

'Everyone thought so,' Justin mumbled. Then he lifted his lips in an unconvincing smile. 'Pretty funny, huh?'

Maybe not. 'Were they counting on this when they put you on Offense?' Daniel asked. 'What does this mean for you and the team?'

'Forget about that, dude,' Justin said. 'Good thing I'm so naturally athletic and gifted anyway, huh?' He smirked, holding up his arm to show off his muscles, and Daniel rolled his eyes. *Typical Justin!* For once, though, Daniel wasn't sure how his twin was really feeling. Was he just putting on a brave face?

'Um . . . are you OK with not having turned?' he asked.

Justin smiled. 'Yeah. Of course. It's all good.'

Daniel studied his face. 'Are you sure?'

'Positive.' Justin nodded firmly. 'But you'll just have to take my word for it, dude. I'd give you a high-five to show there's no hard feelings, but the truth is, I don't think my muscles could take it.'

'OK.' Daniel smiled. 'I'll give you a break, then . . . since it's your birthday.'

'Don't think I'm giving you a break just cos it's yours!'

As they joked and talked and finally caught each other up on everything that had *really* happened on this strange day, Daniel's shoulders gradually relaxed with relief. Sure, he might be a werewolf . . . and his family might have been keeping secrets from him for almost all his life . . . but at least he still had his brother on his side.

Chapter Eight

I am totally OK with this, Justin told himself the next day, for at least the hundredth time since breakfast.

He was running with the football at practice now and, as he felt the good burn of effort in his legs, he put his head down for extra speed and thought: *Everything will be OK now that I know what's going on.*

OK, so he'd thought he was going to be a wolf like his dad, but now he'd be a 'were' like his mom. That was OK. Nothing wrong with being a 'were'. For one thing, Justin could actually go out on a date with a girl on the full moon without worrying about howling and turning furry . . .

Or at least, he *could* if he ever managed to work up the courage to ask Riley out.

He winced at the thought, and barely dodged Kyle's incoming lunge. Darting free, with the ball tightly tucked under his arm, he aimed towards the touchdown line, ignoring visions of Riley . . .

Think bigger than dates, Justin told himself. Hey, there was something even better about Daniel's news! Now, Justin didn't have to *wait* for anything any more! The waiting had definitely been the worst part of the last few days. So really, it was all fine.

Totally fine, Justin told himself, for the hundred and fifth time. *There's nothing wrong with being a regular old human.*

Then Ed Yancey and two other Beasts all piled into him at once. The impact knocked him flat on to the ground and shock juddered all through his body.

Except that everything hurts! Justin thought glumly, from the bottom of the pile of Beasts.

Coach's whistle sounded. 'We're done for the day. Shower off, cubs!'

Biting back a groan, Justin picked himself up and hobbled towards the locker rooms. Across the football field, he caught a flash of bright red hair – his new neighbour Debi, practising with the other cheerleaders. Justin lifted his hand in a neighbourly wave, but she only managed a tight smile.

Head cheerleader Mackenzie Barton's voice boomed through her megaphone. 'Shoulders straight, Debi! Can't you do anything right?'

Ouch. Justin looked away politely, but he couldn't help overhearing as Mackenzie kept yelling.

'Pom-poms higher, Debi! *Higher!* Didn't you hear me? And I want to see a smile on your face as you do it!'

I'm surprised she doesn't whack Mackenzie with one

of those pom-poms instead, Justin thought. *That would sure put a smile on my face!*

It had been bad enough living across the street from Mackenzie for all those years. He couldn't imagine having to take *orders* from her!

Actually . . .

Justin hesitated on his way to the locker room, looking back at Debi and wondering if he should hang around and wait for her to finish cheerleading practice. Maybe he could take the opportunity to put in a good word for Daniel?

He certainly needs the help, Justin thought, and grinned as he thought of Daniel's phone disaster last night.

OK, there were some advantages to being an ordinary human after all. At least talking to Riley on the phone wouldn't make Justin turn wolf!

Just as he thought that, his phone rang. *Uh-oh.* His smile disappeared. *Could she be calling? Now!?*

Justin slumped with relief – and just a bit of

disappointment – when he looked at the screen and saw that it was his dad.

'I need you to do me a favour, bud,' said Dad, when Justin answered. 'Can you pick up Daniel's guitar from the music room?'

'Um . . . sure.' Justin frowned. Since when had Dad been interested in Daniel's music? 'Why?'

'I want him to have it on our camping trip this weekend. You know, so it's not all wolf-stuff.'

Justin muffled a sigh. He had been kind of looking forward to the father–cub trip, when he thought that *he* would be the one going. It was only fair, of course. Daniel deserved the bonding time with Dad, especially since he'd had all of this craziness thrown at him yesterday. Still, it felt weird for Justin not to be the one going off with Dad this time.

Get a grip, cub! he told himself, mimicking Coach's sternest voice. 'Will do,' he said cheerfully.

'Thanks, kiddo. Daniel's off at the store

picking up marshmallows for s'mores, so he won't see you bring it home. I want this to be a good surprise for him tonight, to make up for some of the shock he's been through.'

'Good idea.' Justin hung up, feeling better as he remembered what was really important.

This camping trip wasn't a treat for Daniel – it was a lesson in becoming a wolf. And his brother could use some *serious* help right now.

By the time he'd showered off and gone to the music room, cheerleading practice had come to an end. Justin was just walking out of school with the guitar when he saw Debi leaving her own locker.

Excellent. Now was his chance to really give his brother a helping hand.

Justin waved. 'Hey, Debi!'

She smiled. 'Hey! On your way home?'

'Yup.' He lifted the guitar. 'I just had to get this first.'

Her smile deepened. 'I guess we might as well walk home together, then.'

'Cool.' Justin fell into step beside her, trying not to wince at all the aches and pains from football practice.

As if she'd heard his thoughts, Debi asked, 'Did you have a good practice?'

Justin sighed. Luckily, she was looking at the guitar, and his bruises from the Beasts' pile-on were safely hidden underneath his shirt. 'Ah . . . not too bad.'

'"*Not too bad*"?' She raised her eyebrows at him, grinning as they stepped out the main door on to the broad front steps of school. 'That's not usually how people describe *rocking*.'

For a moment he just looked at her, confused. Then his lips twitched, and he almost laughed out loud in delight. He'd forgotten that the cheerleaders could see the football players' practice. And if Debi wanted to describe the way he'd played that afternoon as 'rocking' . . . well, who was he to argue?

'It's true, I do rock,' Justin said, and he leapt down the last stone step as easily as if he didn't have a single bruise.

I guess my moves were pretty impressive! Justin thought as he landed on the walkway to the main road. His grin broadened as his walk became a strut. *I did make it on to the team even without any werewolf powers. I do rock!*

He could have swaggered all the rest of the way home if a familiar, irritated voice hadn't punctured his good mood. 'So *there* you are, Debi.'

Oh, no. We're being Mackenzinated!

Mackenzie Barton sat on a bench by the walkway, her face pinched, watching a video on her smartphone. Justin heard tinny cheers sounding from it.

'Today's practice,' she informed them haughtily, pointing at the video. 'And it is *not* impressive. Debi, you need to be lighter on your feet!'

And you need to get over yourself, Justin thought, scowling.

Beside him, Debi only nodded calmly. 'Thanks, Mackenzie,' she said. 'I'll work on that.'

Mackenzie blinked, looking startled – and annoyed. 'Well. Anyway.'

'Bye, Mackenzie,' Debi said sweetly, and walked away.

'Wow,' Justin whispered, as he followed her. 'Nice. I would have totally lost it with her if I were you.'

Debi shrugged. 'I've dealt with girls like Mackenzie before. The one thing meanies hate the most is when their targets don't react. So I never do.'

'Huh.' Justin studied her, impressed, as they walked the last few blocks back home. 'Clever thinking.'

Debi was nice, and smart . . . Daniel had made a good choice.

So let's see if I can help him out.

Justin was still trying to think of a good way to bring up Daniel when they reached their block.

If you want someone who never reacts to Mackenzie . . . No, that wasn't right. Daniel reacted plenty to Mackenzie.

You know who else hates Mackenzie . . . No, definitely not. That list was way too long!

If you want someone who could be a real wolf when you need one . . .

Justin groaned as they reached Debi's front yard. *Think, Packer! You're almost out of time!*

Debi tipped her head to one side, curling her long red hair around one finger. 'Do you want to see my new house?'

He let out his breath in a sigh of pure relief. 'Yeah, that would be great.' He definitely needed the extra time.

He was *so* not cut out for this kind of thing! Daniel was the one who was good with words – he even wrote song lyrics. He'd know exactly what to say.

Forget being cool. Just say anything! Justin told himself.

Debi opened the front door, and they stepped into a bright, sunny living room with wide windows. Boxes stood stacked in one corner beside a pale blue sofa and a tall lamp.

'Nice,' Justin said.

'But not exactly the kind of place that would "inspire" you, right?' She gave him a teasing look. 'Based on your tastes, I'm guessing you probably prefer a darker environment?'

'Uh . . .' Justin hesitated, thrown off guard. *My 'tastes'? What's she talking about?* Then he caught himself. *This isn't about me.* 'You know,' he said firmly, 'Daniel's a really great guy.'

Debi let out a startled laugh. 'Um . . . yeah.

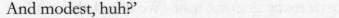

And modest, huh?'

'Yes!' Justin said. 'He's totally modest. Daniel would never tell you this, but Daniel's great at lots of things, not just music. And –'

'*And* he likes talking about himself in the third person,' Debi said, a tremor of laughter in her voice.

She took the guitar from him, looking as if she were about to start giggling. As she set it down, she opened up a small leather case from the side table.

Justin blinked. *Huh, I never noticed Daniel talking about himself in the third person.* Then he winced, realising when it must have happened. *If he did that on their phone call last night, it must have gone even worse than I'd thought! Time for serious clean-up action.*

'Here's the thing about Daniel,' he began. 'He – hey!' he yelped, as Debi took his hand and started buffing his nails. 'What are you doing?'

Debi dropped his hand, looking startled. 'It's

151

just a manicure,' she said. 'We talked about it last night on the phone. Remember?'

Justin stared at her. She and Daniel had talked about manicuring Justin's fingernails? *Seriously, dude?*

She picked up his hand again, shaking her head. 'It's a good thing you've already cut your nails,' she said. 'I don't know how you ever managed to play the guitar with them so long.'

'*I* played – ? Oh. *Oh!*' Justin's mouth dropped open. *She thinks I'm Daniel! Why would she think that?*

Then his gaze fell on the guitar and he understood. *Of course!* Debi had seen him carrying the guitar, so, with them looking identical and everything, she'd assumed he was Daniel. *Disaster!*

'Now, don't worry,' Debi said. 'This won't hurt a bit, I promise.'

She bent over his nails, humming to herself, and Justin squeezed his eyes closed in anguish.

If the Beasts ever find out I've had my nails done, I am so dead.

But there was no turning back. He had spent almost twenty minutes with Debi thinking he was Daniel. If he told her the truth now, she'd be so embarrassed, she might never speak to either Packer boy again. Daniel would kill him if that happened.

OK. So I'll be Daniel. Justin took a deep breath. *It can't be that hard, right?*

'Why don't you tell me more about your band?' Debi asked brightly, as she started on his second fingernail.

'My band . . .' Justin swallowed.

She snickered. 'You can keep talking in the third-person if you like. It's funny.'

'Heh. Right.' Justin swallowed. At least this should be a little easier. '*Daniel's* band,' he said. 'Well, you know, Daniel's band is going to be great. It's called . . .'

153

Uh-oh.

What *was* the name of Daniel's band? Sheepskin? Sheepmouth? Sheepsnore?

I can't believe I've forgotten it. He talks about that band all the time!

If he wasn't enduring an unscheduled manicure for Daniel, Justin would think he was the worst brother in the world.

As it was, though . . . Justin saw the bottle of clear nail polish in Debi's manicure kit and cringed.

After this, Daniel and I are definitely even.

///   \\\   ///

Daniel was working on his math homework in the kitchen when he heard his brother finally arrive home from school.

I can't believe I'm doing homework on a Friday afternoon! Daniel sighed as he finished the fourth equation. If he'd had any idea how long this werewolf bonding trip with Dad would last, he would have put off the work until Sunday, as usual . . . but for all he knew, they might not even get home until Monday morning.

Still, he was happy to set the work aside when Justin walked into the kitchen, waving his empty hands as if trying to shake something off them. 'Late practice?' Daniel asked.

'Worse.' Justin waved his hands accusingly at Daniel, and his fingernails glinted. 'I got these for *you*, Bro. Just remember that!'

'Remember what?' Daniel grabbed one of Justin's hands. 'I don't see anything . . . wait. Did you paint your fingernails?'

'Debi did, thank you *very* much. Because she thought I was you!'

'What?' Daniel stared at his brother.

Justin collapsed into the chair across from him with a sigh. 'It's a long story, dude. But just remember: I did it for you.'

'Did what?' Dread built in Daniel's gut as he

looked at his brother's expression.

By the time Justin finished his explanation, Daniel had his face buried in his arms. 'She thought *I* was saying those things about myself? She must think I'm a total jerk! Am I going to have to talk about myself in the third person from now on?'

Justin shrugged. 'No . . . No . . . Not all the time.'

Daniel groaned. 'Like she didn't think I was enough of a freak already!'

'Oh, get a grip, Daniel –' Justin began.

But Daniel didn't wait to hear his brother's excuses. Leaving his homework behind, he walked out of the room.

He didn't care if his homework didn't get done. At this point, nothing could make this weekend any worse.

It was almost a relief to leave an hour later. By early evening, Daniel and his dad were at Lycan Point, pitching a tent together in the midst of the tall pine trees. The tangy scent of pine needles floated through the air, and birds rustled in the trees as twilight settled around them.

Dad pounded in his last tent pole and stepped back, grinning. 'Isn't it great we can do this father–cub bonding experience together?'

Daniel winced, still hammering his own last tent pole. 'Do you have to call me a cub?' he mumbled.

Dad laughed and ruffled his hair. 'You'll get used to it in no time. You have no idea what a wonderful world you're entering into!'

Daniel sighed as he set down his mallet. *The wonderful world of turning into an animal. Hmm, not sure that I see it!*

'I just have to warn you about a couple of things.' His dad looped one arm around Daniel's shoulder and pulled him over to sit on the rough ground beside him.

Pine needles lay scattered around them, and small creatures rustled ominously in the trees nearby as Daniel waited for his dad's warnings.

'Silver,' Dad said. 'You'll want to avoid that from now on. We're allergic.'

'Got it,' Daniel said and frowned, remembering Debi's necklace. 'Oh, yeah! That makes sense now.' So he hadn't been imagining things – it really *had* caused all his sneezing!

And speaking of Debi . . . Remembering what had happened when they'd talked on the phone, he hunched his shoulders. 'What about the change? How do I stop that happening?'

'Stop it?' His dad shook his head, letting out a surprised laugh. 'Son, the change is the best part! You'll learn to love it – and you'll also learn to control it . . . eventually.'

'"Eventually"?' Daniel grimaced. He could

already feel his nails itching, as if the change had been summoned just by talking about it. 'I want to control it *now*!'

'Well, that's not going to happen. At this age, you'll turn on every full moon and also when you get emotional. But as you get older, you'll learn to turn it off and on at will.'

Daniel dug his nails into the dirt, as if that could stop them from lengthening. 'How long will that take?'

'It depends.' Dad shrugged. 'I'd talked all this over with Justin, so he's had years to practise the exercises for control. It'll take a while longer for you, since you haven't had the chance to prepare.'

Daniel growled. 'So I'll be a freak for even longer.'

Dad sighed. 'Why don't we start working on your special senses? Tell me what you can smell right now.'

Daniel took a deep breath. The sudden rush

of scents was dizzying. 'Well, there are the pine trees, obviously . . .'

'Further off,' Dad said. 'Can you smell the rhododendron bush a half-mile away?'

Daniel sniffed harder. It felt like a thousand scents were all competing to get through to him. 'Um . . . no,' he admitted. 'Sorry.'

'OK. Well, why don't you try listening instead? Tell me when you can pick out the meowing of that cat stuck in a tree in the next town over.'

Closing his eyes as darkness settled around their campsite, Daniel struggled to pick out the sound. In the rush of different noises that flooded his senses from miles around, he couldn't pick out so much as a purr.

Sighing, he opened his eyes. 'I'm sorry, Dad.' He shrugged. 'There's so much out there . . . picking out just one piece feels like trying to find a guitar pick buried in a bag of tennis balls. I can't do it.'

'Oh, well,' Dad said. 'Don't worry about it.' Disappointment flashed across his face so quickly, Daniel couldn't have even glimpsed it without his wolf-vision.

There are some things I wish I couldn't see.

Daniel clenched his teeth. The last thing he wanted was to let his dad down. If he had to be a wolf-freak, why couldn't he at least be an impressive one?

I bet Dad wishes Justin had been the werewolf, after all.

Daniel turned away so Dad couldn't see his expression.

What he saw when he turned, though, made his eyes widen.

'Hey, is that my guitar?'

'I thought it might make you more comfortable to have it along,' Dad said. 'Why don't you show me what you can do?'

'Really?' Daniel blinked. 'But you're not into

my kind of music. You like 'Song to the Moon' and all that other classical stuff.'

Dad lay down on the ground, linking his hands behind his head. 'Just because I'm married to a classical musician doesn't mean I can't appreciate rock – especially when my son is the one who's playing it.'

Wow. Daniel shook his head, amazed. *Dad really is trying to bond with me.*

He scrambled to his feet. 'OK,' he said. 'I'll show you.'

Maybe he wasn't much of a werewolf yet – but Daniel knew what his *real* skills were.

The new guitar was sleek and cool against his waist in the evening air. Daniel tuned it quickly while his dad gazed calmly up at the deep blue sky, and stars began to appear between the clouds.

Then Daniel took a deep breath and let himself go.

He wasn't just practising in his room this time

– he was performing for one of the people who mattered most to him in the world, showing his dad exactly how good he had become. The still night air was the perfect stage, and his dad was the only audience he wanted. Every frustration of the last few days, every moment of embarrassment or fear, was swept away into the music as he rocked out, letting it all pour out of him.

Even when he felt his skin begin to itch, he didn't stop. He just adjusted his grip to use his lengthening fingernails like guitar picks and let the wolf come out to play. For once, the howl that poured out of his mouth felt just right.

It was matched by a howl of delight from his dad – he had turned, too! But his fur didn't look weird to Daniel this time – it felt exactly right for this moment, surrounded by nature. A *part* of nature. Now they were howling together to the music, as Daniel continued to rip out an eerie, haunting melody from his guitar.

The tune had shifted into something new, something that played off all of the sounds his sharp wolf-hearing could pick up in the air for miles around – all that jumble of sound turned into music, gorgeous and new and right. It was the perfect melody to fit the lyrics he'd written two nights ago, the night everything had changed: 'Moonlight Girl'.

And for the first time, Daniel realised exactly who he'd written it for, as he imagined her dancing to the music he played, her red hair glinting in the moonlight.

Of course, he thought, as he howled along to the music of the night around him. *It was always Debi.*

Chapter Nine

It wasn't the most exciting way to spend a Saturday, but with the werewolves in his family off bonding at Lycan Point, Justin headed towards the store to get some candy.

As he passed Debi's house, her front door opened.

'Hey, neighbour!' Justin waved, carefully cupping his hand so she couldn't see his fingernails.

'Hey.' Debi smiled tentatively, then bit her lip. 'Um . . . sorry, which twin are you?'

Justin laughed, then put on a mock-offended expression. 'What, isn't it obvious I'm the cool, athletic one?'

'Sorry, Justin.' Her cheeks had turned pink. 'It's just hard to tell when you're not carrying your trademark football.'

'Or Daniel's trademark guitar?' Justin said, thinking of the mix-up yesterday afternoon. He'd had to scrub and scrub his nails to get all the clear nail polish off them. Then he'd bitten them ragged just to make sure none of the Beasts ever suspected him of even knowing what cuticle cream even was.

'Don't worry about it,' he continued. 'Not many people can tell us apart. Really, it's only Riley who ever –' A shadow appeared behind Debi. 'Riley!'

Justin's voice turned into a yelp as Riley stepped out of the house, smiling.

'Hi, Justin.'

Don't stare, Justin told himself. But how could he not?

Riley's shining blonde hair was tied back in a ponytail, she had three gel pens hooked over the neckline of her tank top, and she was carrying two pads of paper and a thick file folder bulging with notes.

She looked *amazing*.

Justin fell back a step, feeling his cheeks burn. *Thank goodness I'm not a werewolf.* Judging by the way Daniel reacted to Debi, Justin would be hairier than Coach Johnston right now if he had the werewolf gene!

'Are you OK, Justin?' Riley frowned. 'You look –'

'I'm *fine*!' he said – and cursed himself when his voice broke on the words, coming out as an undignified squawk. He cleared his throat. 'I mean . . . everything's cool.' He nodded at the bulging file folder and notepads, trying to recapture his confidence. 'You look like you're planning to take over the world.'

Debi giggled. 'Just the literary world . . . For now.'

Riley nodded, her eyes gleaming. 'We're doing a book presentation together. It's going to be *great*!'

Justin looked back at the pile of notes. *Wow. It's not even* real *homework – it's just for one of her clubs.* 'Are you presenting it tomorrow?'

'Oh, no,' Riley said. 'Not for two weeks. But it's important to be prepared, don't you think?'

Debi only smiled without saying a word. There weren't any notebooks in *her* arms, Justin noticed. *Hmm.*

As nice as his new neighbour seemed, he'd bet anything she wasn't nearly as into this project as Riley was.

But that was exactly what made Riley great: she got so *involved*! She cared about everything. It made her like a light, drawing him in. Which meant he was . . . *a moth?*

Justin took another hasty step back, just in case either of the girls could read his expression. *Think about something else!* he told himself. He saw Debi's gaze land on his ragged fingernails, and he winced. *Remember, you're not supposed to have been the one who talked to her yesterday.*

'So . . . I heard you made the cheerleading team,' Justin said. 'Congratulations!'

Debi rolled her eyes. 'Don't let Mackenzie hear you say that! I'm on the *squad*, not the real team – Mackenzie has made that *very* clear. I won't be cheering unless one of the top girls needs a sub. Mackenzie doesn't want me to get "*above myself*".' She sighed.

'Don't worry about her.' Riley shrugged. 'Mackenzie doesn't like anyone except herself.'

'I think she particularly doesn't like me,' Debi said. 'Maybe it's because I live in her old house?'

'Trust me, everyone except Mackenzie is

169

happy about that change,' Justin said. He squared his shoulders. *Time to make up for yesterday's mistake.* 'I think Daniel said he saw you yesterday?'

Debi's gaze dropped. She smiled mysteriously. 'Mm-hmm.'

'Did you know he was feeling pretty sick yesterday?'

'Really?' Debi stared at him. 'He didn't say a word.'

'If he acted kind of strange, that was why.' Justin nodded firmly. 'He's all better now, though.' *And he won't talk about himself in the third person ever again, I promise!*

'That's good,' Debi said. She was frowning, though, as if she were mentally replaying yesterday's conversation.

Justin stuck his hands behind his back, just in case he'd missed any spots on his nails. *Quick. Get her distracted!* 'You know, speaking of Mackenzie and cheerleading . . . why don't you ask Daniel if he can help make up a new chant for the cheerleaders? That way you wouldn't have to use that awful one Mackenzie came up with.'

'That *would* be good,' Riley said. 'Mackenzie's cheers are legendarily bad.'

'Yeah, the whole team would be grateful,' Justin said. 'And Daniel's an awesome musician – he'll come up with something great. And . . .' Steeling himself, he turned to Riley. *Just act cool, Packer! Act cool!* 'If Debi's too busy with the cheerleading, I could always help you with your book . . . talk . . . presentation . . . thing . . .'

Oh, great. He closed his eyes in agony. *Now she thinks you can't even* speak *English, much less read!*

When he opened his eyes, he caught the two girls giving each other a meaningful smile. His heart sank.

They must both think I'm an idiot. I can't believe I even asked.

'You know what? Don't worry about it,' he

mumbled. 'I'm sure you don't –'

'No!' Riley said. 'I mean . . . ah . . .' She glanced at Debi, who smiled encouragingly at her. 'That would be . . . yeah . . . that would be great.' Her cheeks looked suddenly pinker than before.

'OK,' Justin said easily. 'Cool.'

With an effort, he kept himself from pumping his fist in the air.

TOUCHDOWN!

He was working on a project with Riley!

As he turned to head out to the candy store, he had to stop himself from swaggering. It felt almost . . . kind of . . . like he'd just asked her on a date!

As they drove back into town on Sunday night, Daniel heard his dad humming a familiar song. His lips curved as he recognised the tune.

Dad had been humming 'Moonlight Girl' all weekend. He'd even helped Daniel refine it in a few places, to layer it better. Daniel grinned as Dad turned the car on to their street, still humming.

Daniel had learned a lot about being a wolf from Dad this weekend . . . but he was pretty sure that Dad had learned a lot about him, too.

As Dad parked the car outside their house, he gave Daniel a quick grin. 'Don't look now, son, but Moonlight Girl's across the street!'

'What?' Daniel sat bolt upright, his confidence dropping away faster than light.

Dad was right. Debi was sitting on her front porch, reading a book. There was *no way* he could get out of the car without her seeing him! Daniel let out a yelp of horror that came out as pure wolf.

'Breathe!' Dad said firmly. 'Breathe . . .'

Daniel drew in a deep breath and let it out. He took another breath and slowly, tentatively relaxed.

His skin wasn't itching. There weren't any tufts of wolf-hair on his hands.

Maybe I can learn to control this after all.

'You OK?' Dad asked.

Daniel nodded, still breathing deeply.

'Good.' Dad took another look out the window, and his lips twitched. 'I'd be more than happy to take our stuff into the house, if you have . . . *other* things to do.'

'Thanks, Dad.' Taking one last deep breath, Daniel got out of the car. He stood on the kerb, preparing himself.

Debi hadn't looked up to see him yet, so he had a moment to get this right. When she did look up, he wanted her to see him walking across the street in a cool way.

He shook his head at himself. *Yeah, right. Like* that's *going to happen.* After all the ways he'd made a fool of himself in front of her so far, he'd be lucky if he didn't trip and fall flat on his face while she was watching!

Just please don't let me look like a doofus, he thought.

Daniel looked at the road between him and Debi's house. Suddenly it looked like a castle moat, or maybe even an ocean, huge and impassable.

Maybe it would be safer to just try walking across the street in a normal *way this time?*

He set one foot off the kerb – then jumped back. *What* is *my normal way of walking?*

'Daniel?' Debi had looked up from her book and was watching him. 'Is everything OK?'

Daniel winced. 'Absolutely.' He crossed the street, somehow managing not to trip as he walked. 'How are you doing?'

'Oh, I'm fine!' She smiled and patted the porch beside her, making a space for him to sit. 'I'm just reading this book for Riley's book group.'

Daniel sat down, careful not to bump against

her. The feeling of being so close to her made his skin tingle, but it wasn't out of control yet.

Breathe . . . breathe . . .

He forced himself to look at the cover of her book instead of staring down at her hair as it brushed against his shoulder. 'I've never heard of Count Vira.'

She shrugged. 'I thought I'd give it a try, since everyone back in Franklin Grove seemed really into this series. It's pretty good, but not exactly my thing.' She slid a look up at him, her blue eyes so vivid, they made his breath catch. 'What about you? What kind of books do you like to read?'

'Um . . .' Daniel hesitated. Did graphic novels really count? They *should* count . . . but what if Debi didn't think so? Would she think he was dumb? But on the other hand, if she *did* think they counted, that would make her even cooler!

But then again . . .

For once, he was actually grateful to be

interrupted by Mackenzie Barton, who turned the corner of their street and rollerbladed towards them, wearing full cheerleading uniform and scowling intently.

'Oh, no,' Debi muttered. Then she put on a polite smile and waved. 'Hi, Mackenzie! Can I help you with anything?'

Mackenzie slammed to a halt outside Debi's house and looked at her with outright disgust. 'Are you *reading*?' she asked.

'Um . . .' Debi looked down at the book in her hand and raised her eyebrows. 'I was.'

'What good do you think *that* will do you? We have a game to cheer at tomorrow – and you're *reading*?' Mackenzie snorted. 'Ugh! No wonder you're so heavy-footed.'

Still grumbling, she spun around and rolled away, her hands on her hips.

It took all of Daniel's concentration to keep his growl inside his chest and his nails from growing. *Breathe . . . Breathe . . .*

'I am *so* glad she's moved away,' he said, clenching his hands to keep control. 'When I think she used to live here, and now we get to have *you*.' He gulped as he caught himself. 'I mean –'

Debi's eyes widened. For a moment, neither of them moved.

Did I just tell *her how I feel?*

Daniel swallowed again. He could feel his pulse against his skin. His mind had gone completely blank.

Then Debi put one hand on his arm, and he froze. 'Can you help me with something?' she asked.

'Sure! Of course. Yes! OK!' He slammed his mouth shut before he could keep going. *I think she understands by now . . .*

'Good,' Debi said. Her chin was up, and she looked determined. 'Because that did it. From now on, I am not going to let Mackenzie have everything her own way any more. I need to borrow your song-writing skills.'

'My song-writing skills?' Daniel blinked. *She hasn't even heard 'Moonlight Girl' yet!*

She nodded. 'Will you come in for a bit and help me write a cheer? I want to write something so good, it'll blow Mackenzie's out of the water.'

'Got it.' Daniel stood up, feeling a moment of disappointment as her hand dropped away from his arm. It was probably for the best, though; his face had started tingling the moment she'd laid her hand against his skin.

Squaring his shoulders, he pushed down his emotions and followed her into the house.

I can do this, he thought. *All I have to do is help her against Mackenzie . . . without letting her see the wolf.*

////   \\\\   ////

By lunchtime the next day, Daniel was starving. He'd eaten a huge, meaty breakfast, but his stomach had still growled for hours. Even as he saw his brother coming towards him, he couldn't wait to pull out his sandwich from his locker. 'C'mon, let's head to the cafeteria.'

Justin shook his head, looking nervous. 'The Beasts'll expect me to sit with them, and I need to talk to you alone.'

'OK.' Daniel leaned back against his locker and pulled out his first sandwich. 'But I've got to get started. Talk to me while I eat.'

Just the smell of the corned beef in his sandwich made him feel faint. He shoved it into his mouth as Justin came to stand beside him.

'It's today's game!' Justin hissed. 'Dude, I am freaking out. We're supposed to play the Tigers after school, and there is no way I'm going to be able to perform to the level all the Beasts – and Coach – are expecting!'

'I'm sure you'll be fine.' Daniel spoke around his sandwich, because he couldn't stop eating. *Why didn't Mom pack five of these instead of two?* 'Look,' he continued, wiping his mouth with his arm, 'you're a natural athlete, and no one's figured out the truth about you so far, right? The Tigers won't notice any difference either.'

'Maybe . . . I don't know. Ahh!' Justin banged his head against his locker. 'I hate this! How can I do this without wolf powers?'

Daniel checked left and right to see if anyone had heard. Luckily, no one had. He squeezed Justin's shoulder encouragingly. 'This is just . . . stage fright. Mom says everyone gets nervous before a performance.'

'I guess.' Justin sighed. 'Will you be there for the game?'

'At least for the first half,' Daniel said. 'It depends how long the game goes on. I might need to skip out of the last half to take care of final auditions.'

Justin grimaced. 'It's going to be a long game, Bro. With the amount of time I'm expecting to be down on the turf, injured, there'll be plenty of time outs.'

'Ouch.' Daniel winced sympathetically. It was hard to concentrate, though, since his super-sensitive wolf hearing was picking up every conversation in the hallway around them. Even as he tried to listen to Justin's worries about the game, he heard guys halfway down the hall, talking about the math test they'd just taken. He heard Riley at the very end of the hallway, saying to another girl from the book society, 'My cousin is staying for the weekend, so we're going to go see the new Jackson Caulfield movie and –'

'Bro?' Justin said. He waved a hand in front of Daniel's eyes. 'Hey, are you still listening to me?'

'I am!' Daniel said. Silently, he added: *I'm just*

listening to everyone else, too.

'Are you sure?' Justin frowned. 'You look kinda –'

Just then, Riley came up behind Justin. 'Here's Riley,' Daniel said, and Justin jumped back, swiping hastily at his hair.

'Hey, guys!' For once, Riley was only carrying three books. Her hair was loose around the shoulders of her preppy button-up blouse. She shot a quick look at Justin, then turned to Daniel. 'I just wanted to ask about this afternoon's sing-off. Is there anything I need to know?'

'Nothing in particular.' Daniel shrugged, pulling out his second sandwich from his backpack. 'Just be yourself, sing your best.'

'I'm sure you'll be great,' Justin said.

'Are you really sure?' Riley smiled teasingly at Justin. 'How do you know? You've never even heard me sing.'

'Well, yeah, but . . .' A wave of red swept up

Justin's face. 'I'm sure you . . . I mean, you are . . . you know . . .'

Daniel bit into his sandwich, smirking. It was good to see he wasn't the only Packer who got tangled up around girls.

From his perspective, though, Justin didn't have anything to worry about. As Riley listened to Justin's stammering response, she casually twirled a shining strand of her long blonde hair around one finger. Daniel had read all about that in one of his mom's magazines. When a girl played with her hair while she talked to a boy, it was a way of letting him know through body language that she had a crush on him.

Definitely.

On the other hand . . . Daniel frowned, pausing mid-bite to think it over. Riley was so gawky and fidgety anyway, maybe playing with her hair didn't mean anything after all. Did she always do it, no matter who she was talking to?

He'd never noticed her doing it before, but . . .

He peered harder at her over his sandwich.

She turned. 'Is something wrong, Daniel?' Before he could answer, she let out a startled laugh. 'Wait a minute. Is that beef in your sandwich? I can't believe it. I thought you never ate red meat.'

'Um . . .' *Oh, no. What am I supposed to say?* Daniel felt his teeth and nails start to grow with sudden panic. *I can't let her figure this out. What do I do?*

He heard his dad's voice coaching him. *Breathe . . . Breathe . . .*

'Something is up, isn't it?' Riley frowned, stepping closer. 'What's wrong? Are you feeling sick?'

Daniel stared at his brother, trying to send him a message with his eyes: *Help!*

'I think Daniel just choked on his sandwich,' Justin said, and gave Daniel a meaningful look back. Daniel hastily started coughing, playing along with the excuse. Justin gave him a hefty pat on the back then shifted between him and Riley to block her view. 'So, Riley, what are you doing this weekend?'

'Me?' Riley blinked rapidly – or was she batting her eyes? Daniel couldn't tell from where he was. 'I'm completely free. All weekend. No plans whatsoever! Nope!'

Daniel stopped coughing. 'I thought you were going to the movies with your cousin.' He'd just overheard her say this, hadn't he?

Riley peered round Justin to look at Daniel. 'How did you know that? The only person I've even told was Malinda, and that was just two minutes ago.'

'Uh . . .' *Oh, no. Mistake!* Daniel tried to think of an excuse, but his brain wouldn't function. *Breathe! Breathe!*

In the end, all he could do was offer a shrug – which came off more like an exaggerated shiver.

Great. As Daniel watched Riley walk away a few moments later, still looking suspicious, he finally let out the breath he'd been holding. 'I can't let her into the band!' he hissed to Justin. 'She's way too observant.'

'Dude?' Justin looked at him and shook his head. 'Just remember: I let Debi give me a manicure – *for you*! You owe me – and that means you *have* to let her in the band, no matter what.'

He wanted to help his brother out, he really did. But what if Riley discovered the truth?

Chapter Ten

At half-time in that afternoon's game, Justin sat slumped on a bench in the locker room. He couldn't even think about girls, rock bands, or anything else but his total physical misery. Around him, all of his teammates, Beasts and humans alike, hooted and punched each other, revving up for the next quarter. Justin just let it all pass over his aching body and tired mind.

What was the point in joking around? The Tigers were ahead of the Wolves by ten points already, and Justin knew it was his fault. He just didn't see anything he could do about it.

It wasn't just that he was exhausted from

training with the Beasts – he was flat-out terrified of getting pounded in a pile up and really hurting himself.

'Come on, cubs.' Coach's whistle blew at the entrance to the locker room. 'We can do this. Just get out there and show those Tigers what real wolves are made of!'

As the rest of the team ran out of the locker room, hooting and growling with determination, Justin couldn't even bring himself to join them. He just sat slumped on his bench, watching them go.

What was the point? He wasn't a wolf. He wasn't really supposed to be here. If Coach or any of the Beasts knew the truth about him, they'd kick him off the team.

He thought of all the years of waiting as Dad told him about the change that would come this year. *It wasn't supposed to be this way.*

'Justin?' Daniel's voice finally broke through

Justin's haze of self-pity.

Justin blinked and looked up. His twin must have come in without him even noticing. Now Daniel was standing over him, staring down at him.

'What's wrong with you?' Daniel asked. 'Why aren't you out on the field? Everyone's waiting for you!'

'I know.' Justin sighed. He couldn't even move to shrug. 'I can't do it, man. I literally cannot move my legs.'

Daniel sat down on the bench beside him, frowning. 'I may not know much about football, but I know the Wolves can't win without their star sprinting back.'

Against his will, Justin let out a snort of laughter. 'That's "running back", dude. Not "sprinting back".'

'See?' Daniel grinned and shoved his shoulder playfully. 'You know everything about football.

That's why they need you out there.'

'What they really need is someone to take my place,' Justin said. 'Someone who actually *has* wolf powers.' Then inspiration struck with a bang. He sat bolt upright, ignoring all his aches and pains.

Daniel edged away. 'I don't like the look on your face, dude. Whatever you're thinking –'

'This is perfect!' Justin was already scrambling to unlace his football boots. 'There's plenty of time before the auditions. Who would know the difference? No one!'

'No!' Daniel stuck his hands out in front of him like a stop sign. His face was filled with horror. 'No way,' he said. 'Justin, this is crazy. Trust me. I don't care what you say, you are not talking me into this one!'

/// \\\ ///

I can't believe I let Justin talk me into this one! As Daniel made his first catch, he heard the roars of approval from the crowd in the football stadium and stared at the ball in his hands, dizzy with disbelief.

His brother's boots felt heavy and awkward on his feet, and the padded uniform hung strangely on his shoulders. Worse yet, everything looked weird and distorted through the bars of the football helmet. *I so don't belong here.*

Even as Daniel thought that, though, he remembered the misery on his brother's face. He'd never seen Justin looking so defeated. *I can do this,* he told himself. *For my twin.*

Plus, Justin had absolutely promised: all Daniel had to do was run and not get hit.

As Daniel prepared to charge forwards with the ball, he heard a familiar sound breaking through the noise of the crowd.

'Wolves on top, we're number one! Growling 'til the game is done!'

It was the cheer he'd helped Debi make up. Debi was there with the other cheerleaders, cheering them on – and the new cheer was so much catchier than Mackenzie's usual chants. Soon, everyone in the stands was chanting it, too.

The sound was like a shot of adrenaline into Daniel's veins. *I am a werewolf. And I can do this!*

Growling with sheer excitement, he went for it – and as he charged through the opposing team members, before falling at the twenty-yard-line, he realised: he was actually *good!* It was the first time he'd done anything that really called on his werewolf powers, and it was fun!

Kyle Hunter called a time-out. Daniel eagerly returned the Beasts' high-fives, enjoying being among other guys like him.

Unfortunately, his werewolf powers didn't include the ability to decode football plays.

'Thirty-four! Sixty-eight! Twenty-nine! Dakota!' Kyle bellowed.

Whatever that means . . . Daniel did his best to

play along, but a few minutes later, Kyle signalled to him.

'All yours, Packer,' Kyle yelled. 'Pine Wood tradition – new cubs get to call one play in the second half of their first game.'

'Uh . . .' Daniel stared at Kyle, as their team-mates waited expectantly. *Just go for it!* he ordered himself. *How bad can it be?* 'Ninety-eight . . . Seventy-eight . . . Fifty . . . six . . . And, uhm . . . Cincinnati?'

A long pause amongst the team. They stared hard at Daniel.

'Genius!' Kyle roared his approval, and the other Beasts joined in enthusiastically.

Daniel grinned weakly. *What did I even say?*

Whatever it was, it seemed to work.

A moment later, he found himself in open space. Kyle had the ball but couldn't pass to any of the usual receivers. He hurled it downfield to Daniel.

The ball soared through the air. Daniel jumped high, feeling werewolf strength propel his legs. Laughing out loud with exhilaration, he reached out, grabbed . . .

. . . and burst the ball with his super-long nails.

Oops!

'Time out!' The referee's whistle blew, and the game went into an extended time-out while the organisers went in hunt of a new ball.

'Doofus!' Kyle loped over to Daniel and swiped at his helmet. 'Come on, Justin. Didn't you even think to cut your nails before the match?'

'Uh . . . I guess not,' Daniel said. His eyes flickered over to the giant scoreboard at the far end of the field where a clock ticked away the seconds.

Uh-oh. The audition was due to start in five minutes. 'Just gimme a minute,' he said. 'I'll run back to the locker room and cut them now.'

Kyle sighed. 'OK, but hurry! You need to be back by the end of this time-out.'

'I will be,' Daniel promised.

It's time for Justin to get back into this game.

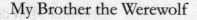

Ever since his twin had left, Justin had been sitting on the floor with his head tipped against his locker, trying not to think about what was going on out on the field without him. When he heard the sound of running footsteps, though, he looked up.

Daniel was already shedding the big padded uniform as he lunged towards the bench. 'It's time, dude. I've got to be at the audition *now*.'

Justin sighed. 'Is the game over?'

'Not by a long shot.' Daniel shook his head as he kicked off the football boots. 'You'd better hurry. They're expecting you out there *now*.'

'Whatever.' Justin sagged. 'I give up, man. I'm not a wolf. I can't –'

'Stop it.' Daniel grabbed his shoulders. 'Look at me, twin.'

Reluctantly, Justin met his twin brother's eyes. Daniel's expression was fierce with belief. 'So what if you're not a werewolf?' Daniel asked. 'You're still a great football player. We both know that!'

'But I was supposed to be a wolf! They all expected –'

'Forget about them,' Daniel said. 'Don't you remember what you told me last week?' He shook Justin by the shoulders. 'You are the *king* of football! Remember?'

Justin's chest tightened. 'But –'

'Have I ever told you a lie?' Daniel asked.

'Never,' Justin said. He'd had to keep the truth about their family secret from his brother, but Daniel had never once lied to him.

'Then you know what I'm telling you is true. You can do this!'

Justin took a deep breath as his twin's confidence soaked into him. 'I can do this,' he said. 'I can still play football.'

'You know you can.' Daniel held out the football boots, and Justin saw his name picked out in large letters: *PACKER*.

They belonged to him. And so did this game.

Justin pulled on the boots and headed back out to the field.

///   ///   ///

Daniel came skidding down the hallway just in time. Milo and Riley were both waiting outside the auditorium for their final audition. Daniel could hear the other band members warming up inside.

'Hey, guys.' He led the two singers into the auditorium, pulling out his guitar from its case as he walked.

One of the music teachers, Ms Milanovic, stuck her head in the door just as he jumped on stage. There were six or seven choral society members standing behind her. 'Can we sit in on this audition?'

'Sure.' Daniel shrugged as he started to tune his guitar. 'Why not?'

'"Why not"?' Milo scowled as he stepped on stage. He marched over to Daniel. 'No one told me I'd have an audience! I'm not prepared for this!'

'You're absolutely right.' Riley gave a mischievous grin. 'Just imagine! A rock band playing in front of an audience? Who could have prepared for that?'

As Milo scowled harder, Daniel had to bite back a laugh.

I forgot how funny Riley could be.

She didn't take any nonsense, either. She'd be perfect for the band . . . if only she wasn't so observant.

Nathan handed out sheet music to Riley and

Milo as Daniel finished tuning his guitar. 'Why don't you guys take a minute to get acquainted with our new song?' Nathan said. 'It's called "Moonlight Girl". We'll play it once through as a band, so you two can get the melody, and then you'll both sing it as your audition.'

'What?' Milo scoffed. 'Sorry, are you serious? You really expect me to perform a song I've only known for five minutes?'

Otto stopped setting up his drum kit to give Milo a narrow-eyed glare. Then he and Nathan both looked meaningfully at Daniel. The message in their eyes was clear: *What a jerk!*

Daniel winced. *Come on, Milo. You're making it very hard for me to persuade the others to pick you.* 'Don't worry,' he said. 'Just relax and do your best. We aren't expecting a polished performance.'

'Whatever,' Milo mumbled.

Beside him, Riley was reading the lyrics. After a moment, she looked up and gave Daniel a look that felt uncomfortably knowing.

He gulped and looked back down at his guitar, hoping she hadn't figured out that he'd written the song about Debi . . .

Then Otto set a pounding beat on the drumset, and it was time to launch into the song.

'A smile bright as stars . . .'

Singing wasn't Daniel's strongest suit, but he took the lead vocals for this run-through. With the power of the band behind him, his confidence lifted. Otto's drums were like a heartbeat, pouring energy through his veins, while Nathan went wild on the guitar. It was by far the best Daniel had ever sung – especially during the howling section that closed out the number.

'Whoop whoop!' Riley cheered, clapping hard and joined by enthusiastic applause from the audience.

Milo just stared at Daniel, bug-eyed. 'I thought this was supposed to be a *rock* band, man. I'm not into sappy stuff.' He curled his lip as he looked down at the music in his hands. 'Who is this "moonlight girl" anyway?'

Feeling heat rise to his face, Daniel stepped back, letting Nathan and Otto defend the song. Unfortunately, as he looked away from Milo, his eyes met Riley's – and her smile was *too* knowing.

'Don't worry,' Riley said, cutting across the argument. 'If you need to hear the song again, Milo, I'll gladly go first. You ready, guys?'

Nathan grinned at her, flinging his purple and black hair out of his eyes. 'Absolutely.'

Otto set a beat, and Riley prowled to the front of the stage, all her usual gawkiness dropping away from her as she shook out her hair. Now that the music had begun, she didn't look like an awkward, preppy girl any more. She looked like a rock star. It was a total transformation – and as she launched into the song, her voice rich, confident and full of power, Daniel had to admit: she was *nailing* this audition.

Riley didn't just sing 'Moonlight Girl' – she took it to a whole new level. Her voice turned the band into a unit, stronger than they'd ever been before. And when it came to the end of the song, Riley's voice harmonised perfectly with Daniel's on the howls, as wild and free as if she were a wolf herself.

Otto threw down his drumsticks with a clatter before the song was even finished. 'Man, Riley! You rock!'

As the students in the audience stood up to cheer, Riley laughed delightedly. She swept a graceful bow – without tripping – then gestured for Milo to take her place. 'Your turn.'

'Great,' Milo muttered. He was scowling as he stepped in front of the band.

Still adrenalised by the last performance, Daniel mentally urged Milo on. *Come on, Milo.*

Knock it out of the park!

He couldn't imagine anyone singing 'Moonlight Girl' better than Riley had just done. But if Milo didn't do just that . . . then Daniel's biggest secret was going to be in serious danger of coming out.

Justin was huddling with the rest of his team at the five-yard line when he heard the cheer begin on the other side of the field.

'Wolves on top, we're number one! Growling till the game is done! Wolves are fierce and never tame. With claws and heart we'll win this game!'

Wow. That doesn't sound like any of Mackenzie's cheers! Justin thought. But if it hadn't been written by Mackenzie . . . then that meant Debi had gone for it. She'd been brave enough to stand up against Mackenzie after all of her bullying . . .

Justin could be that brave, too.

That's right, he told himself, as the cheer continued and the crowd chanted along. *Who cares if I'm not a werewolf? I belong on this team.*

The only difference between him and the Beasts was that, unlike them, he'd *earned* his way on to the team without any extra werewolf powers to help him . . . and that made him even more awesome, didn't it?

Right at that moment, as he heard the crowd chanting the new cheer as clearly as if they were chanting right to him, Justin made a resolution: *From now on, I don't care what anyone else thinks I should be. I'm going to prove I have exactly what it takes, just the way I am!*

'Right, wolves,' Kyle barked. As quarterback, he was leading the huddle. 'Packer's gotten us to the five-yard mark, but we only have ten seconds left on the clock. What we need right now is a field goal. As long as we get those three points, we'll draw the game and –'

'Not good enough, captain.' Justin shook his head and looked Kyle eye-to-eye, letting his own strength and confidence shine through his gaze. 'We should go for the touchdown and the win.'

Kyle frowned. 'But if we don't make it –'

'We'll make it,' Justin said. 'We're better than the Tigers, and you know it. We're too good to settle for a draw.'

'You know what, Packer? You're right.' Grinning widely, Kyle clapped Justin on the back. 'Spoken like a true Lupine!' He raised his eyebrows behind his visor. 'You want the ball?'

'Absolutely,' Justin said. Adrenaline was pumping so hard through him that when Kyle high-fived him, he didn't even feel the pain. Nothing could hurt him right now.

The team took their places on the field, and the referee's whistle blew.

'Hike!'

Kyle faked throwing to a receiver. Then he handed it off to Justin.

I can do this.

Head down, Justin barrelled through the Tiger's Defense with one last burst of purely human strength. Just three more yards, then two more – *one* . . .

Justin launched himself over the line and landed with a thump.

'Touchdown!' the referee roared.

He'd made it!

Justin's teammates piled on to him, whooping with wild joy. For once, Justin didn't care about a single bruise. He just lay on the green of the football field and grinned up at the blue sky above him.

The whistle blew for the end of the match.

Pine Wood had won. And so had he!

Chapter Eleven

Less than twenty minutes after he'd arrived at the sing-off, Daniel was leaving the auditorium with his bandmates, on his way to make a very difficult decision. When he saw Debi walking down the hallway, though, her jacket slung over one arm and her face filled with misery, he forgot about everything but her.

'Hey!' Daniel hurried over to her, leaving Otto and Nathan behind. 'Didn't I just see you on the field? Isn't the game still going on? What are you doing here?'

Debi stared at him. 'What were *you* doing on the field? I thought you'd be preparing for your auditions.'

Oops. 'Um . . .' Quickly, Daniel searched for a distraction. 'So how did the new cheer go down?'

He'd expected her to cheer up at that, but instead, Debi let out an unhappy sigh. 'Too well.'

'"*Too* well"?' Daniel shook his head. 'What does that mean?'

'It means, Mackenzie took me out.' Debi slumped. 'The game's still going on out there, but she sent me home.'

Daniel felt a growl build up in his chest. With an effort, he forced it down. 'Mackenzie's obviously feeling threatened because you're the better cheerleader.'

'Sure.' Debi shrugged. 'That doesn't help me though, does it? Maybe we shouldn't have written the cheer.' She looked down. 'If I'd just let Mackenzie have her way again . . .'

'Absolutely not,' Daniel said. 'You deserve

your spot, and you should fight for it. You can't just let her win!'

'Maybe not.' Debi sighed and looked up at him, her blue eyes lost. 'It's just . . . a little hard to remember that right now.'

'Come on.' Daniel reached out to touch her arm, then stopped, curling his fingers back as he realised his fingernails had grown with his anger. 'Hey, Riley's in the auditorium. Why don't you go hang out with her? Otto and Nathan and I just have to go deliberate.'

'OK.' Debi nodded, some of her usual energy seeming to return. She pulled on her jacket. As she slid it over her shoulders, the motion pulled her silver necklace free of her collar.

Daniel lurched back. *Breathe . . . Breathe . . .*

Gritting his teeth, he remembered Dad's lessons in control. He didn't care what it took – he could *not* embarrass himself in front of Debi again!

'Daniel?' She was watching him, looking worried now. 'Are you –'

'I'm fine,' he said, backing away. 'See you soon.' Daniel nodded, breathing through his nose. Then he turned towards the room where Otto and Nathan were waiting for him. It was time to make a final decision . . . and, unfortunately, he didn't think Debi was going to like their decision any more than he liked her silver necklace.

It took almost half an hour for Daniel to talk the others round to his point of view.

'I don't know. But if you're really sure, man . . .' Otto finally muttered.

'Positive,' Daniel said.

Nathan only sighed, letting his purple and black bangs fall over his eyes as if he couldn't bear to watch it happen.

They walked out together into the hallway and found that everyone else was waiting there for them. Riley and Debi stood together chatting away, while Milo stood further down the hall, playing a game on his smartphone. With Daniel's sharp werewolf hearing, he could hear everything Riley said as she gazed down at Debi's silver necklace.

'. . . that is so beautiful. I want to get one just like it!'

Ouch. Daniel stiffened his spine. *See? We made the right decision.* The last thing he needed was a silver necklace in his own band!

Still, he swallowed hard when Nathan gestured for him to step forwards. It was only fair: he was the one who'd forced this decision on the others, so he should have to be the one who announced it.

But he could hear the reluctance in his own voice as he spoke. 'Hey, guys. We've finally made our decision.'

Riley spun around so fast, her legs tangled. Debi caught her before she could fall, then took

212

a discreet step to the side, as Milo slithered up next to Riley.

'Well?' Milo asked. His chin was held at a confident tilt. 'Let's get it over with, OK? I want to start rehearsing.'

Riley didn't say anything. But the expression on her face made the words stick in Daniel's throat.

I have to do this, he told himself. *And if she asks why we've chosen Milo . . . I'll give her a good answer. It'll sound reasonable. It will.*

But nothing about it *felt* reasonable as he saw the desperate hope – and fear – in Riley's face. He'd never seen Riley scared before.

She *really* wanted this. And when he thought about the way she'd acted on stage – the total transformation – he knew why it was so important to her.

Riley might be the queen of organisation, but that didn't mean she was confident about herself.

Daniel had known her ever since kindergarten, and he knew the insecurities hiding behind her whirl of activities. She might be pretty and smart, but he knew how shy she was inside, and how self-conscious she felt about her height. But on stage, she was graceful. Poised. She didn't trip. It was the first time he'd ever seen the 'real' Riley unleashed. And as Daniel looked at her now, he realised that he couldn't turn the real Riley down.

Maybe it was stupid . . . and he knew it would definitely put his secret at risk . . . but it was right. She was the better singer, in every way. She deserved the spot. He couldn't take it from her.

'So,' he said, and cleared his throat. 'We've chosen Riley as our lead singer. Sorry, Milo.'

'What?' Milo gaped at him, even as Debi gave a shriek of delight and jumped at Riley for a hug. 'What are you talking about?' Milo demanded. 'You can't choose her over me!'

'We already did,' Otto said, and clapped

Daniel on the back. 'Sorry, man. She just fits the band better.'

'Welcome to *In Sheep's Clothing*, Riley.' Nathan held out his hand, which Riley shook, beaming, as Debi stepped back.

'This is a fix!' Milo threw up his hands, slamming his smartphone against the closest locker. 'You won't get away with this. You haven't heard the last of me! I'm going to start my own band, and our wrath will be *righteous*! We are going to destroy *In Sheep's Clothing* like a storm cloud of vengeance!' With a bellow of rage, he stomped down the hallway away from them.

Daniel rolled his eyes, as his bandmates laughed.

'*Definitely* the right choice,' Nathan said.

'Absolutely.' Otto nodded respectfully to Riley. 'Glad to have you with us, Riley.'

'Me, too,' Riley said. She was beaming with relief, her hair messy for once from Debi's hug.

'But Daniel . . .' She pulled him aside as his bandmates headed back into the auditorium. 'What made you choose me? I *know* you – I could tell you were hoping for Milo to win.'

'I know *you*, too,' Daniel said, and sighed. 'You're not a pretender, like Milo. Those songs sound so good when you sing them because you're being yourself on stage. You belong there.'

Riley's face lit up. "You mean that?"

'Definitely.' Daniel smiled. Then he glanced over to Debi who was fingering her necklace, and he coughed. 'Um, but there is one condition . . .'

Riley looked worried. 'What's that?'

'You can't ever wear silver. Not in rehearsals and not on stage. OK?'

'What?' Riley stared at him. 'Why would that matter?'

'It . . .. wouldn't look right when we're gigging.'

Riley said nothing. She just looked at him like he'd gone crazy.

'It's bad luck!' Daniel said desperately. 'I'm superstitious about silver. Dumb, huh?' He tried to laugh, but it came out like a yelp.

Riley shook her head at him, frowning. 'There is something really weird going on with you, Daniel Packer. I can tell.'

'No, there's nothing, I swear –'

'Something weird,' she said with a nod, 'and I'm going to find out what.'

Before Daniel could respond, Debi joined them, her eyebrows shooting up in reaction to Riley's last words. 'Something weird, huh? Well, trust me, I grew up in Franklin Grove – nothing could be weirder than that!' She gave Riley another hug. 'I'm so happy for you. And for you!' She turned to Daniel. 'You guys definitely made the right choice. I can't wait to see you all in action.'

'Me, too –' Daniel began. Then he choked as Debi threw her arms around him.

It's just a friendly way to congratulate me, he told himself, as he put his arms around her to return the hug. *Just like the hug she gave Riley.*

Still, he closed his eyes to savour the feeling. Tingles raced through him, and he ordered himself: *Breathe . . . Breathe . . .*

This time, though, the tingles weren't in reaction to her necklace. They were definitely all Debi.

Justin stepped out of his house the next evening and took a long, deep breath in satisfaction. His dad was already standing by the backyard grill, cooking up an evening barbecue to welcome Debi's family to the neighbourhood. Steaks sizzled on the grill for the Lupines and other meat-eaters, while vegetarian burgers and shish-kebabs cooked nearby. Daniel stood by the meat-eaters' grill, already chomping down his first burger while he talked to Debi, and looking happier than Justin had seen him in days.

'Hey, Justin.' A familiar voice spoke just behind him.

'Riley!' Justin spun around, almost tripping with surprise as he took in the sight of Riley, standing just inside his house and carrying a microphone on a long metal stand.

'What are you doing here?' he asked. Then he winced. 'I mean – it's good to see you! You're here for the barbecue, right?'

'Actually, I came to play in my band.' She grinned and pointed with her microphone to her shirt. For once, she wasn't wearing a preppy vest or a blouse. Instead, she wore a black T-shirt with a familiar, rocking logo and the large words: *In Sheep's Clothing*.

It should have felt weird to see her in such a different outfit . . . but it didn't. It felt right. Riley looked happy and confident and *amazing*. In fact . . .

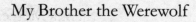

'. . . Um, Justin?' She coughed, breaking his trance. 'Can I come through?'

'What? Oh! Yes.' Justin finally realised he'd been blocking the doorway as he'd stood staring at her. *Doofus!* 'Yeah. Great! Come in. I mean, out,' he said, as he moved out of her way. 'Great that you're in the band. *In Sheep's Clothing.* Um . . .'

He cringed.

Stop talking now! Please, mouth, stop talking!

She was smiling, though, as she stepped outside. 'I'm glad you think so. And actually . . .' She flushed. 'Do you think you could help me set up my microphone? I've never done it before.'

'Of course!' Puffing up his chest, Justin led her across the backyard to where the drum kit was waiting. As he set up the microphone, he caught Daniel's eye across the backyard.

Thank you, he mouthed.

Daniel toasted him with his burger, sending a piece of lettuce flying. Luckily, Debi's head was turned away as the lettuce flew straight past her ear. Justin smirked as he saw his brother's eyes widen in horror at the near-disaster.

He didn't know what it was that had made Daniel finally decide to let Riley in the band, but wow, was he grateful . . . especially because the band was going to need to do a lot of rehearsing from now on, right? And they'd probably need a streetie – err, roadie – to carry their gear . . .

Especially for their lead singer.

'Why are you grinning?' Riley asked.

'Oh, no reason.' Justin wiped the smile off his face. 'Just looking forward to the show.'

'Oh, yeah?' She put one hand on her hip challengingly. 'Do you think you'll really be able to handle watching me rock out? It won't be too weird for you?'

Justin snorted. 'Trust me. At this point, *nothing* is too weird for me!'

'What do you mean?' Riley gave him a questioning look.

'Never mind.' Justin smiled. 'I can't wait to hear you sing. I know you're going to be great.'

Riley made a nervous face. 'I hope you're right.'

'I *am*,' said Justin.

And he was. Twenty minutes later, he stood next to Debi, listening to *In Sheep's Clothing* perform the song Daniel had written with Dad up at Lycan Point that weekend . . . Justin instantly worked out exactly who his brother had written the song for.

Hair like fire, huh? He hid a grin as he looked between his brother and Debi.

'So,' he whispered to Debi, 'what do you think of the song?'

'It's fantastic!' She bounced on her toes with enthusiasm, matching the rhythm of the music. 'The whole band is great, isn't it? And I just love "Moonlight Girl". Do you know who it's about?'

Shrugging, Justin took a big bite of his veggie burger to keep himself from giving any secrets away. *Daniel will kill me if I let Debi know he has a crush on her.*

But as he watched his brother rock out, Justin made himself a promise: he was going to make sure his twin got all the happiness he deserved. After all . . .

. . . His smile widened as he saw Riley tip her head back to howl . . .

. . . Justin owed Daniel big now. And – werewolf or human – Justin would always have his twin brother's back.

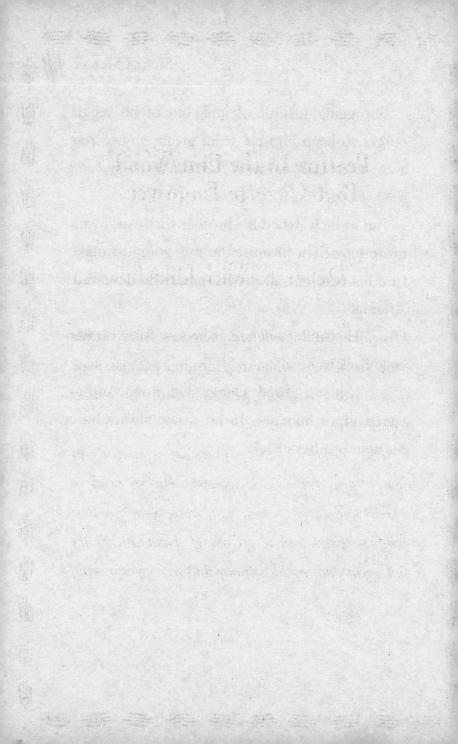

Feature in the Pine Wood
Post-Gazette-Enquirer

Repartee With Riley!

Hey, Pine Wood People! It's your fave feature in the Pine Wood Post-Gazette-Enquirer *(only one week to go for votes on whether we should shorten the student paper's name . . . Hint-hint!)*

This month's student interview, conducted by yours truly, features the awesome Packer twins — Daniel and Justin — and, well, when those two start talking, things tend to get out of hand. Here's the full uncut and unedited transcript for your enjoyment!

Riley Carter: Are you ready for some repartee with Riley?

Justin Packer: 'Repartee'? That sounds like a martial art.

Daniel Packer (puts hands up): I surrender already!

Riley: No, no, no – it just means, 'to talk'.

Justin: You could have just said 'talk'.

Riley: But that would be a lame way to start an interview.

Justin: Yeah, you're so right. Of course it would be.

Daniel (laughs): But explaining the meaning of the word 'Repartee' is much better to start an interview.

Riley (clears throat): So, a new school semester, a new year: 9th grade – how does it differ from 8th?

[*The twins share an awkward look*]

Riley: What was that look?

Daniel: Nothing. 9th grade is, uhm . . . it's got . . . bite.

Justin: The classes have really gotten harder.

Daniel: Yeah, *that's* the biggest difference – there's a lot of homework to get our teeth into.

Riley: Lots of changes – Justin, you made the football team. AND you scored a touchdown against the Tigers. How great was that?

Justin: It was . . . OK.

Riley (sighs): That's it? 'OK'? Justin – we're going for 'school-spirit' here. And as the team's star chasing back –

Daniel: *Running* back.

Riley: – yeah, that – you should be more enthusiastic! The cheerleaders are going to have a *very* hard time performing cheers about the 'Shrugging Back' who's not impressed with himself.

Justin: That's actually a relief.

Daniel (laughs): '*Shrugging Back*'. I'm going to remember that one!

Riley: Talking of cheerleaders, do you have a message for them? Any cheerleaders in particular you would like to mention?

Daniel (Chokes and splutters)

Riley / Justin: Are you okay?

Daniel: I'm fine, sorry. It's nothing. I'm fine.

Justin: I would like to thank all the cheerleaders for supporting the team. They do a great –

Daniel: I would too! I would like to thank the cheerleaders too. They're great. Really, I think that some of them – one in particular . . .

Just . . . thanks.

Riley: Oooookaaaaay. But what about the rest of the game? Did it live up to your expectations?

Daniel: It was tough, and scary at times —

Justin: Uhm, dude . . .

Daniel: – Uh . . . I really enjoyed *watching* my brother play football. I can only *imagine* what it was like to be *on* the field, actually playing. I have *no* idea, because I have *never* played football, ever. Justin – what was it like to be *on* the field? You know, since you were the one *actually* playing.

Justin: Erm . . . tough and … scary at times . . . But it was a real rush.

Riley: So, Daniel, is that where you were all afternoon, while I was waiting patiently for my audition?

Daniel: Erm . . . Well . . .

Justin: Hey, Riley, how did it feel to get the lead singer role in Daniel's band?

Riley: Amazing! I get *such* a buzz from performing. Don't think me a colossal nerd, but when I sing, I kind of . . .

Justin: What?

Riley: . . . it's silly.

Daniel: You can tell us.

Riley: You'll think I'm weird.

Daniel: We already think that.

Justin: But in a *good* way. Right, Daniel?

Daniel: Oh yeah, totally. The 'good' kind of weird. Like us.

[*The twins share another look*]

Riley: OK, seriously – you guys need to stop doing that. Either tell me what the secrets are, or stop being all *furtive*!

Justin: Sorry. No more secret looks. Next question.

Riley: Daniel, do you get nervous when you perform?

Daniel: Terrified. But, it's my dream to be a rock star, so I have to get over that. If I want to record songs and play concerts when I grow up, I'll have to fight the stage-fright. That's my dream – travelling the world, playing my songs to fans. I get so excited when I think –

Riley: Are you OK?

Daniel: Yeah, why?

Riley: Well, you're scratching at your arms quite a lot.

Daniel: Oh, I . . . hadn't noticed. I guess even the thought of playing big shows makes me . . . umm . . . nervous.

Justin: You're not getting *too* nervous, are you bro?

Daniel (examines his fingernails): No, I think I'm OK.

Riley: There's that look again.

Justin: Sorry.

Riley: And you think *I'm* weird. Sorry, guys, but I think that's all the time we have for this interview. It's going to be great when it's printed.

Justin: You need to edit this *carefully* before it goes into the *Post-Enquirer-Gazette*.

Riley: *Post-Gazette*-Enquirer.

Daniel: Whatever. You promise?

Riley: I promise.

EGMONT PRESS: ETHICAL PUBLISHING

Egmont Press is about turning writers into successful authors and children into passionate readers – producing books that enrich and entertain. As a responsible children's publisher, we go even further, considering the world in which our consumers are growing up.

Safety First
Naturally, all of our books meet legal safety requirements. But we go further than this; every book with play value is tested to the highest standards – if it fails, it's back to the drawing-board.

Made Fairly
We are working to ensure that the workers involved in our supply chain – the people that make our books – are treated with fairness and respect.

Responsible Forestry
We are committed to ensuring all our papers come from environmentally and socially responsible forest sources.

For more information, please visit our website at www.egmont.co.uk/ethical